I0818066

Romulus Escapes

A post-apocalyptic novel by

William Mays

Romulus Escapes

ISBN 978-1-7334696-7-8

For more information, contact William Mays
Mays Publishing.
Books@mayspublishing.com

Original Cover by Alexis Mays Harborth

Printed in the United States of America
ISBN 978-1-7334696-7-8

DEDICATION

I dedicate this to our son for our discussions of science, our daughter for her cover designs, and my wife for the close reading of the final draft.

Special thanks to my critique group: David Welling, Melissa Algood, Carla Conrad, Clare Hart-Polumbo, E. Paige Burks, and Louis Epstein. You couldn't ask for a better group.

CHAPTER ONE

Romulus had a scalpel in his hand when the notification popped up in his display. RUST. He was a Fax—a machine—and his mechanical problems had steadily worsened in recent years. Not wanting the nurses to suspect, he dialed some arrogance onto his normally bland expression and started the surgery.

The patient was a Real—a human—whose VR implant had stopped working. The interface lay under a patch of synthskin on his temple. Romulus cut through and found the problem. One of the transistors had burned out. He removed it, installed a new one, and sutured the tissue back, finishing the procedure in less than thirty minutes. A little more arrogance inadvertently worked its way onto his face as he strutted out of the operating room.

"Wake up and smell the hydraulic fluid," JOAN, his internal assistant, said. She existed only in his metaverse. They could hear each other, but no one else could. "You may have fooled the nurses, but don't try to fool yourself."

"I did that surgery in record time," Romulus shot back. "I'm as good as I ever was."

"You need a complete overhaul," she yelled. "You are an old, rusting Fax. The Reals will recycle you if they figure out how many problems you have. You are forty years old. That's thirty-three years out of warranty."

"How do I afford a complete overhaul? You know I am short of coin."

"You have to beg Rhymin' Ryan to finance it."

"I hate that guy. And I haven't even paid off my last loan to him. He'll tack on refinancing fees and aging-Fax surcharges."

"You have no choice. Your ratings have been trending down over the years."

"I am still the best. Reals from all over the world come to me."

"You are at 4.76. Ten years ago, your ratings were at 4.97. You're only as good as your last surgery. Your problems will catch up with you. When things fall apart, they fall apart fast. What if some rust clogs your lines while you're cutting into someone?"

She was right. She was almost always right. "I guess I have no choice."

The next six surgeries went by without incident, but during the last one, a gallbladder removal, another notification popped up. BATTERY. It hadn't been holding a charge lately. That was something else for Ryan to finance.

Thankfully, there was nothing scheduled after the gallbladder. He stepped out of the operating room and was about to clock out when General Martin, the Supreme Leader of The Hospital, marched down the hall with a group of soldiers in jeans and Stetsons.

They stopped in front of Romulus. "I need to talk to you, boy," he said in his distinctive drawl.

This was bad. General Martin only spoke to you if you were in trouble. Romulus snapped to attention and saluted. "Yes, sir, General Martin. What do you need, sir?"

Martin was scary. He had piercing blue eyes, a cross tattoo on his forehead, and a sneer so permanent that it looked like a tattoo. He wore a big red Stetson and a matching red western shirt with pearl snaps. "The ga damned Rogue Faxes are attacking. There will be casualties. You got to stay."

"Sir, I've been here forty-eight hours straight. I need

to charge my battery."

"Are you questioning my order?"

"No, sir."

"I am a Real and your Supreme Leader. You are a Fax. You may look like a Real, but you aren't. A Fax's priority is what?"

"To obey."

"So, obey your programming."

"But I need a quick charge, at least, if I'm going to function properly."

Martin snickered. So did the soldiers. "Yes, yes, you are old. Maybe you should ask the Fair Fax Bureau about getting a new battery."

The last thing any Fax dared do was go to the Bureau. You could end up sentenced to clown torture. "Oh, no, I don't want to do that."

"Okay. Get a quick charge and report to East Wing."

They marched on, and Romulus trudged past a kidney repair center, a TruSnak™ dispensary, a spare parts market, and up two flights of steps to a charging chair that wasn't on the map. The Hospital was a behemoth few could navigate, but Romulus had worked in it all his life and didn't need to look at a map. Besides, the map only showed you what Martin wanted to show you.

The chair was in a quiet hall in Recycling Wing 3. It had been there from the beginning when Romulus had just come off the assembly line. His first assignment was to help repair Fax parts in Wing 3, and he fondly remembered sitting on that chair.

He sat and selected double quick charge, then blinked to bring the notifications to full screen. It showed him seventeen microunits over brown rust oxide limits, worse than ever. He'd set up a fake rust profile that sent false data to the server, making him appear healthy.

Had they found out about that? Was that why

Martin had shown up?

To get through the extra shift, he released some TruSnak™ from his reservoir. TruSnak™ was the lifeblood of all Faxes. It brought all his mechanical, hydraulic, and electric systems into harmony. It would minimize the impact of the rust and help preserve his battery levels.

As the sustenance moved through him, he retreated into the favorite scene in his metaverse: a beach with white sand. JOAN built sandcastles. She had black braids, black glasses, and a black bathing suit.

A sailboat glided across glittering blue water; the sun was warm on his synthskin, and the sand felt good on his toes. He enabled his favorite mix track: DJ Fax playing RoboSlick music, a pleasing combination of clanging industrial sounds laid over a hard bassline and a 140-beat-per-minute drum track. Nothing went better with a day at the virtual beach than soothing music.

He couldn't relax, though. General Martin had spoken to him. He'd probably figured out about the rust and would sell him off for parts. Romulus's programming told him to accept anything a Real did, even recycling.

But he didn't want to die.

"Don't get upset, Romulus," a voluptuous blond avatar said. She sat on a towel next to him as she always did when he went to the beach.

"But why didn't they just arrest me? That's what usually happens. They arrest you, and no one ever sees you again. Why didn't he do that?"

"Oh, who knows? Come on. Let's swim."

They ran across the sand, she in her string bikini and he in his Speedos, and dove into the crystal blue water.

When they manufactured him, all Faxes came off the assembly line with thin, lanky bodies, white hairless synthskin, and blond hair. They all had the same parts, including private parts, because that allowed for the cheapest manufacturing. Romulus had extra computing components to make him a surgeon, but that had left no room for pleasure modules to enable sexual performance.

In his metaverse, everything worked. The touch of her synthskin excited him.

They swam so far that he couldn't see the shore.

"We're escaping," he said. "We don't have to live our lives the way the Reals want. We can have freedom."

"Yes. Yes."

Suddenly, she punched him in the side.

"Why are you doing that?" he asked.

"You are out of time, Romulus."

It wasn't the avatar, and the voice wasn't coming from his metaverse. It was General Martin.

CHAPTER TWO

Romulus opened his eyes. Martin stood above him and leaned down until that hateful, weathered face was only inches away.

"They're unloading the ambulances now. Our troops need you. Get up."

Martin had changed into his formal uniform—white Stetson, white silk shirt with pearl snaps, and white jeans. In contrast, Romulus wore the same thing every day: the Fax uniform of an orange tunic over black stretch pants.

Martin held a Fax prod and poked Romulus in the side. It sent a sharp burst of electricity through him. "I said, get up."

Romulus shuffled down to East Wing. There were injured soldiers on gurneys, and the freight elevators at both ends creaked open to bring in more wounded.

One gurney held a soldier with a bullet to the chest. There was no sign of life.

Romulus looked at the nurse and shook his head. "This soldier has passed away. I certify him for composting."

He moved to a warrior Fax. Wires and tubes stuck out of a massive, jagged hole in his chest. The central pump was exposed and oozed hydraulic fluid. While Faxes were expendable, they were still valuable property. A bullet had cracked the metal case of this one.

"Are there replacement pumps?" Romulus asked.

"No," the nurse said. "We are out. Supply chain shortages. What is your decision?"

"I certify this Fax as unrepairable. Send him to recycling."

The next gurney held a Real with a blood-soaked shirt. It was a fancy black western shirt with pearl snaps.

He was a Metroplex Cowboy, one of the elite fighters from Dallas. What was he doing in Corpus Christi?

Martin came up behind Romulus and whispered in his ear. "Take care of this one first. And don't say anything to anybody about him."

"Operating Room One," Romulus yelled to a Fax nurse.

Romulus followed the gurney, cut the shirt off the Cowboy to reveal an abdominal wound, and found the right renal artery spurting blood. He clamped both sides shut and sutured them back together. The bullet lay close to the kidney, so he plucked it loose from the tissue. The soldier would survive but wouldn't be back in action anytime soon.

After treating a dozen more patients, his rust notification kept popping up, his TruSnak™ levels were getting low, and his battery was losing power faster than it should. He felt a clink in his chest. His system had shifted to battery-saver mode.

There was only one more patient: a sixteen-year-old Real with a head laceration. Blood covered his head and dripped on the linoleum, but the bullet didn't penetrate the skull. It had knocked the VR implant out of alignment, however. He released a little more TruSnak™ into his system and cut through the synthskin patch on the forehead. He had done so many virtual reality repairs that he hardly thought as he worked. His hands knew what to do.

A message appeared in his display. *Requesting permission to enter your metaverse.*

In his rear-facing camera, Romulus saw Remus a

few feet behind him. They had come off the assembly line right after each other. Romulus was only a few minutes older. Remus had never developed top-notch medical skills and always got in trouble. While Romulus looked the same as ever, Remus looked different, as most Faxes did as they aged. His synthskin was blotchy and wrinkled, and the right side of his mouth drooped.

Romulus granted permission. "Where did you come from?"

Remus looked over at JOAN. She was still building sandcastles and paid no attention to them.

"They just released me from detention to help with the casualties," Remus said, turning back to Romulus. "I came to warn you that you are in great danger. General Martin is out to get you."

"Why? I'm a good surgeon."

"You are too good. That is the problem. You have the healing hands."

Romulus looked down at them. "They have memory. Distributed processing. I hardly need to tell them what to do."

"You are more talented than any Real. That is why you are a threat. I'm not kidding you. You are in great danger. There is only one option. Resistance. You must join the Rogue Faxes if you want to live."

The Rogues were Faxes who disobeyed their programming and ran off to Mathis Swamp.

"I am not political. I like being a surgeon. I help people. I'm no Rogue."

Remus shook his head, exited the metaverse, and left the operating room.

JOAN started in on him right away. "That malcontent is nothing but trouble, but something is happening. General Martin showed up, followed by Remus. Clock out now and go to Rhymin' Ryan's. Get as much work done as he's willing to finance. And then go home to your cubicle and don't leave until you go back on shift."

"Right."

He clocked out and went into the hall. Martin and the soldiers were waiting for him. "Romulus, I need you in Critical Ward Seven. We're short-handed up there."

"But sir, I've got to get some TruSnak™ and a full battery charge."

"No, we need you in Seven."

It was hard to argue with the Supreme Leader, but he couldn't stop himself. "I might make a mistake in my current condition."

"Obey your programming, now!"

Romulus trudged to the elevator. When the doors opened, stagnant, foul-smelling water spilled onto the floor. It came from leaking pipes on the upper floors. Black mutant worms, some as long as six inches, slithered out with the water.

Not trusting the elevator to work properly, he took the stairs up to Seven. His circuits complained, and he released more TruSnak™ to get through it. His legs wobbled, and he felt—sluggish.

Somehow, he put in another nine hours. There was no end of patients to see, and no other surgeons were on duty. By the end, he was struggling to focus on what the appropriate treatments might be, and he wasn't sure he was making the best choices.

Suddenly, General Martin materialized in a hologram. Since both Reals and Faxes had VR implants, television sets were unnecessary. This signal was beamed directly to everyone and appeared as a hologram.

"My fellow Corpus Christians, I'm addressing you from Critical Ward Seven."

He appeared to be in the ward but couldn't be because that's where Romulus was, and there was no sign of him or his entourage. It had to be a staged green-screen event. While things often didn't work in Corpus Christi, the fake images always worked. The avatar of Honey McSweet, the voluptuous blonde Fax newscaster, stood beside him. "Can you tell us how the war with the Rogues is going?" she asked.

Martin stood in front of a steam table and served barbecue brisket to injured soldiers.

"We got those sumbitches on the run. We have the power of Christ behind us. When you have Jesus, no one can stop you. We are out looking for TinKan right now."

A mugshot of the burly Rogue leader, TinKan, floated next to them. He was the same model as the Warrior Fax Romulus had just treated.

"When we find him, you can be sure there will be a heck of a clown torture party."

"That is something we can all look forward to," Honey said, rubbing up against him.

The image of the critical ward disappeared, replaced by the video of The Corpus Christi Anthem. Hundreds of white-skinned ranchers with assault rifles marched toward The Hospital. A deep-throated singer twanged, accompanied by banjos, fiddles, harmonicas, and steel guitars.

We lived in trailers
And were hay bailers.
The Fat Cats in DC
Screwed us with glee.
We prayed to Jesus
And he lifted us.
We took up arms
And fled the farms.
Tired of pity
We took the city.
Corpus Christi, oh Corpus Christi
When I think of thee
My eyes get misty.

Romulus knew every frame, lyric, and close-up of the white-skinned Reals conquering Corpus Christi after the fall of the United States of America. The square-jawed men had halos around their heads, and the busty blond women cradled blond babies to their bosoms.

There was a different version on ALT>FAX, a feed that was supposed to come from a city that used to be Chicago. It showed images of white Reals brutally clubbing and shooting brown-skinned Reals as they conquered the city.

Romulus figured neither version told the full truth. He had always dreamed of seeing the world, finding the truth, and living where he could be free.

The song ended; the holo disappeared.

Four soldiers came up to him. "Follow us," one said.

They led him down a series of halls to a room with cameras. Martin and Honey McSweet stood in front of a green screen, but there was no barbecue or injured soldiers.

"I need you down in The Basement," Martin said.

"I can't do it," Romulus pleaded. "I need to charge my battery. I may make a mistake. I need to get off shift."

Martin's eyes glowed. The soldiers turned on their Fax prods so high that the tips glowed. "Obey your programming, Romulus. Follow orders."

CHAPTER THREE

"But not the basement," Romulus pleaded. "I'm a surgeon."

"Your job description includes other duties as assigned."

"I've never worked there. I save lives. You can't put me down there!"

"You're getting to be a real smart ass. It's smart-asses like you who disobey their programming and run off to join the Rogues."

"I am not interested in the Rogues. My battery is at twenty percent. My circuits are not working properly. I might make a mistake."

"War is hell. Are you disobeying an order?"

"No, sir."

"All right, that's what I want to hear." He smiled big and showed shiny, white teeth. Like most Reals, he had many artificial parts. His mouth assembly was a Fax part, which accounted for the teeth looking so good. He came up to Romulus, put his arm around his shoulder, and pulled him off to the side. "Listen, we are extremely short-handed," he said in a soft tone instead of his usual harsh voice. "All you have to do is certify them. You don't even have to examine them."

"Not examine them?"

"They've all been examined. All we need is your

approval. We need a Fax of your stature to approve the action."

A Fax of my stature! Romulus thought. Martin had never been nice to him, much less complimented him. "Yes, General Martin, I'll get right to it."

Not wanting to share an elevator with worms, he started down the eight flights of steps.

"Well, this is quite an insult," JOAN said. "Asking you to work the Basement."

"He said I was a Fax of stature. He was nice, and I loved the compliment. Besides, what can I do? An order is an order, and he is the Supreme Leader."

"Watch out. Don't make any mistakes."

"I know."

The stairwell wasn't in any better shape than the elevator. Its ancient LCD lights flickered and buzzed. The pipe railing was rusty. The cement steps had cracks because of the shifting foundation.

One step cracked under him, and hunks of cement fell to the landing below. He grasped the railing, but it pulled loose from the wall, and he nearly tumbled.

He finally reached the Basement. The hallway had cinderblock walls that might have once been white but had long since turned yellow in some spots and brown in others, and there were numerous water stains. The ceiling had exposed pipes and cables. Water dripped down through one of the flickering overhead lights.

He typed his ID number into an old-fashioned physical keypad to enter the ward. The tumblers whirred and cracked and then stopped. Like so much else in The Hospital, it was malfunctioning. He entered his ID twice more, and finally, the door creaked open.

The Basement was vast, with rumbling generators and compressors. An arrow appeared in his display, guiding him from patient to patient. His software identified the rotten-egg odor that Reals found unpleasant. As the years passed, he, too, came to view it as undesirable.

There was no staff, no nurses, no orderlies. A warning in his display said there were high levels of airborne flesh-eating bacteria. He would be careful not to nick or scratch himself. His synthskin was prone to infection.

He recognized the Warrior Fax who had been brought in with a hole in his chest. Romulus checked him one last time. There was no CPU activity. Even if they could bring him back with multiple surgeries and replace his central pump, his files would be hopelessly corrupted, and nothing would remain of his personality.

The determination ledger popped up in his display. It said, *Recommendation: Recycle.*

Romulus approved the recommendation.

The floor was dirty and wet. All the water leaking from everywhere in The Hospital wound up there. It mixed with the blood and hydraulic fluid, forming a sticky sludge on the floor. The mutant worms scurried around. There were so many that he stepped on them even though he tried to avoid them. One bit his boot and then scurried away.

He kicked them out of the way and moved to the next patient: a Brown Real farm worker. A thresher had lopped off his right arm, and his family had bandaged him in the field before bringing him in. The infection had spread throughout his body, and he was delirious. No medicine was available to Brown Reals unless they qualified for BrownCare, which this man had, but the deductible was so high that he had received no treatment.

The determination appeared.

Recommendation: Dream-laced fentanyl and composting.

It was the only option. With the dream-lacing, even if he had any sentience left, he would drift into pleasant fantasies. Then, when he died, he would be used as soil for the vegetable fields. In research on ALT>FAX, Romulus had learned that in the old days of the United States, everyone got a funeral, and many were embalmed and put in caskets. What a strange custom. Now, only high-ranking Reals got funerals.

And so it went, patient after patient. He had trouble focusing, and he felt pain. The Reals had built pain sensors into Faxes so the prods and other torture instruments would control them. The more his battery and TruSnak™ levels went down, the worse he felt. Videos played from his memory. The Corpus Christi Anthem looped into a sitcom from ancient times about a woman named Lucy. Giant spiders jumped out at him. They were so real he ducked.

Fortunately, everything was clear-cut: each patient was dead or nearly dead. He moved as fast as he could, approving each recommendation, barely looking at the details.

At the end of a long line, an old woman lay motionless on her back, her eyes shut, her arms to her side. The recommendation was the same as the others: *Dream-laced fentanyl and composting.*

He blinked to connect to her data. There was nothing except that her name was listed as "Jane Doe." That was the default server setting for an unidentified female Real.

His central pump clanked, and pain shot through him. He needed to certify her for composting and get out of the Basement.

The only problem was that she was alive. Her breathing was shallow, and her vitals were weak. But she was nowhere near dead.

It didn't matter. She probably had some disease and would be gone soon.

He was about to approve the recommendation when he saw that she gripped a long-stemmed red rose in one hand. Roses were rare and expensive. Only important people got roses.

The smell of the flower triggered images of

bouquets and songs about flowers. His simulation software showed that she was beautiful in her youth, and he imagined that they cavorted over dunes and splashed in crystal blue water.

Martin's holo appeared in front of him in a signal directed only to his VR implant. "What are you doing, Romulus?" His tone was friendly, but there was an edge to it.

"This patient is alive. There has been a mistake."

"Mistake? What are you talking about? The analysis has already been done. I need you to certify this patient for dream-laced fentanyl and composting."

"But she's not dead."

Martin's smile faded. "It is not your job to question your role."

"And she is beautiful."

Martin's mouth dropped open in shock. "Beautiful? She's old."

"Her hair and skin are gorgeous. She is so well-preserved that she must be important. See how neat she looks. She takes pride in her appearance. It's obvious. And someone gave her a rose! There must be a mistake. We need to send her back for further evaluation. Her name isn't even right. It's listed as 'Jane Doe.' We have to figure out her name and ID number."

Martin's mouth gaped open in shock. "Oh, my God, Romulus, you are messed up. Much worse than I thought. It's almost like you've fallen in love with her."

Her eyelids fluttered open. Romulus edged forward. She looked up at him and grasped his hand. Her flesh felt warm, as human flesh always did, a good two degrees Fahrenheit warmer than his circulating fluids.

Her eyes fluttered shut, and her hand slipped from his.

"See," Romulus said. "She's very much alive. We need to examine her more."

"I don't know what you're talking about."

"She opened her eyes and grabbed my hand. You saw it."

"No, I didn't see a thing. I think you are malfunctioning and imagining things. We have given this patient enough time. We are fighting a war. Do your duty. Certify her."

This is what it was all about. It was a setup. Martin had overworked Romulus so that he wouldn't question the recommendation. He was going to blame Romulus for the woman's death, and then they would recycle him. Since he would die no matter what he did, he felt rebellious. He would do the right thing.

"I will not certify her for composting."

"What?"

"I won't do it."

"I'm giving you an order," Martin said.

"No, I won't do it."

Martin's eyes opened wide in rage. Romulus had never disobeyed an order. No Fax disobeyed an order from The Supreme Leader and lived.

"I'm giving you one last chance, Romulus," Martin screamed. "Certify this patient for composting."

"No."

"You are about to cross a line, Romulus. There will be no going back."

"Fine."

"Certify her," he screamed, his eyes bulging and flashing red, his mouth drooling. "If you don't do it, I will send soldiers down there with Fax prods.

"No, I won't do it."

"What do you think you are? A Real?"

"No, I'm someone who's tired of getting pushed around."

"Those Fax prods will do more than push you around. You'll be a quivering mass of circuits, and then we'll recycle *you*."

"You were going to do that anyway."

Martin looked at him for a long time. He looked so mad that Romulus thought his head might explode. Finally, his rage lessened, and he smiled big. His fake teeth glistened.

His holo disappeared.

"What are you doing?" JOAN screamed. "You have gone crazy."

"When it's over, it's over. He was going to recycle me no matter what I did. I might as well try to do the right thing."

"No. Your mind isn't working right. Do what he says. Certify her. You may still be able to save yourself. The situation will look different after your overhaul."

CHAPTER FOUR

JOAN was annoying him, so he muted her. He accepted his fate. As Faxes learned and aged, they sometimes developed weird fixations. There had been a Farm Fax, who claimed to talk to cotton plants, and a Warrior Fax, who began making elaborate origami sculptures. Both were recycled.

Had he developed an odd fixation for the old lady, or were his logic circuits temporarily malfunctioning? It didn't matter. He had passed the point of no return.

He moved on to the last patient, a teenage Real, a Blue Urchin. Romulus had seen him in the TruSnak™ district. The name in his record was "Abraham Blue Seventeen." He had dark skin and wore a tattered blue T-shirt as required by law.

Sores covered half his body.

The recommendation was the same as for all the others: *Dream-laced fentanyl and composting.*

Notifications in motion-activated holograms floated all around him. "Highly Contagious," they said in red. Romulus had soft tissue that made him susceptible to disease. All he had to do was approve the recommendation and avoid the risk. But Abraham was nowhere near dead.

He blinked to connect to the boy's profile. The data confirmed what Romulus suspected. It was flesh-eating bacteria, one of the new sexually transmitted variants that were epidemic in Urchin Park.

The teenager opened his eyes. "It was just a few sores the other day," he said.

His arms and legs were strapped to the bed to keep him from trying to escape.

"Please help me."

If he had come in sooner, the infection would not have progressed to this stage, but urchins feared the system more than disease and never came in until it was too late. This was all part of the grand plan. If urchins were afraid to come for help, then they would die, and costs would be kept down. The boy didn't even have TexasHealth—as worthless as it was.

The *irony* was that antibacterial medicine could cure him. Soldiers often came down with the condition after visiting prostitutes at Urchin Trailer Park. There was a ready supply of doses in the upper wards.

"Please don't kill me," Abraham said. "Please, help me. I'm but a poor Blue Urchin. I was born in the back of a trailer. My momma was forced to be a sex worker. I had no advantages, no help. I grew up under a trailer. I ate food out of a garbage can. I know I should have gone to an approved sex facility, but I was in love and had no money. I have no business being in love, living, or having any pleasure or joy, but I couldn't help myself. Can you understand how I feel? There is no fun and no hope."

Romulus completely understood what it was like to have no joy or hope.

"I couldn't help myself," the boy concluded.

Romulus couldn't help himself either. By helping the old lady, he had probably already doomed himself. He would help Abraham.

He messaged the boy. *I'm granting you permission to enter my metaverse.*

The boy accepted. "I'm going to help you," Romulus said, motioning to a door near them. "That leads to the outside. Wait for me out there. I'll bring you some medicine."

Abraham looked at him in disbelief. Romulus looked around to see if anyone was watching. No one was. There were cameras and microphones everywhere, but he didn't care. He opened a window in his display, accessed The Hospital server, and navigated to the Basement cameras. He paused them all for two minutes. The red indicator lights turned off. If anyone reviewed the footage, it would look like there had been no motion to activate the recording.

He untied Abraham's straps. "There are some orange toxic waste barrels out there. No one should be around them. Hide behind them. I'll bring you medicine for your sores."

Abraham still didn't move.

"Go!"

Abraham jumped off the gurney and ran to the door. Romulus turned off his locator in case soldiers were coming to arrest him. He wanted to check on the old lady, but he knew that's where the soldiers would be waiting for him.

To get through the next few hours, he released more TruSnak™. A warning notification flashed.

Your reservoir is down to five percent.

He worked his way through the Basement, ducking behind compressors and generators, and took the back stairs to the fourth floor to the medicine cabinets holding antibiotics. He stopped in the hall outside the alcove where the drugs were. Seeing no one in front or behind, he sent out a jammer signal instead of trying to disable the cameras. It was quicker than turning them off via the server.

The lights on the wall-mounted cameras started blinking red, indicating they were malfunctioning and sending alerts to the server. He ducked inside the alcove. There was a camera on the wall above the cabinet. It, too, blinked. He would only have a minute before the system reset, but that was all he needed.

Stealing from the dispensary was a severe crime that led to summary recycling, but Romulus was already violating so many rules that it didn't matter. He accessed the cabinet's virtual keypad and entered his ID. There would be a record, but so many had access that it would be impossible to tell who had taken the antibiotics.

The cabinet door popped open. He grabbed three single-dose auto-injects. They were broad-spectrum and might not be optimal for some of the variants of the flesh-eating bacteria, but they would probably work.

CHAPTER FIVE

With the single-dose auto-injects in his pocket, he walked back down the hall as the cameras shifted from blinking red to solid red. The system had reset, but he was in the clear! He felt a crackle of joyous, low-voltage electricity surge through his system.

What a thrill to disobey cruel and stupid orders!

The next problem was how to get to Abraham. It was too risky to go back through the Basement. The soldiers would be looking for him.

He went down an empty, unused hall to the stairs that led to the old underground parking garage. Whole sections of The Hospital were empty. Corpus Christi had expanded too rapidly and had been in recession for years.

Inside the stairwell, a red-and-yellow plastic barricade blocked him from going lower. Thick plastic sheets hung from the ceiling. A red warning holo flashed as he drew closer.

"This exit is not available now," a sweet-voiced announcer said. It was Honey McSweet. She had been getting a lot of airtime because she was dating General Martin.

What was going on? He stepped close to the railing to peek through a gap in the plastic sheets.

"Please, step back," Honey said in a not-so-sweet voice.

Boy, they didn't want anyone snooping around. That made him even more curious, but he stepped back. If he persisted, the server might identify him and send out an alarm, and he didn't want any soldiers to know where he was.

A holo map appeared. "Enter your destination," Honey commanded. "The best route will appear in front of you, and I will guide you every step of the way."

Romulus stepped back until the holo disappeared and walked up the stairs one floor to a wiring closet. It had a sheet-metal crawl space that connected to every part of The Hospital. During his early years, hospital expansion was non-stop. Most of the Reals felt claustrophobic in the crawl spaces, but Romulus didn't mind and helped with much of that installation. He knew them better than anyone and enjoyed navigating the numerous twists and turns as he remembered his youth.

He made his way down to the parking garage and then to an old skywalk. No one used it anymore because the contractor, a cousin of General Martin, had used faulty materials. The roof leaked, rats took up residence, feral cats followed the rats, and there were more mutant worms.

Stepping carefully and quickly to avoid the snarling and scurrying residents, he turned into another hall. He was surprised to see sheets of particle board blocking his way forward. He checked his internal map to see if it had any information.

It didn't show the hall at all.

Somebody at a very high level had deleted the hall from the map.

What were they trying to hide?

The particle board was nailed to a frame. One spot at the bottom was not nailed flush. He fit his hand through and, with his great physical strength, pried the nails loose a little at a time. The board was so flimsy it wanted to crumble, but he was careful because he didn't want anyone to see that something was wrong.

Nail by nail, he pulled it away from the frame until he could squeeze through. When he got to the other side, he pulled it back in place so that, from a distance, it would appear undisturbed.

In front of him, there was a long hall alongside what had once been the Wellness Clinic, where they had sent the terminally ill for dream-laced fentanyl. Instead of doors and windows leading into the clinic, there were floor-to-ceiling sheets of particle board.

Mechanical sounds came from the other side, growing louder as he approached. There was riveting, gears grinding, and conveyor belts whirring.

Two men were talking. He pressed his ear against the wall and filtered out the lower frequencies to hear the conversation.

"So, how fast can we get this up and running?"

It was the unmistakable twang of General Martin.

The next voice was not familiar. "We should be able to start mass production in a few weeks."

"I'm counting on you and the rest of the team. If we pull this off, the Metroplex will make us a full partner. We'll be big. Do you understand? Big!"

"I will not disappoint you, sir."

"And you've taken care of that other matter?"

"I went right down to the basement. We could not find Romulus. It appears that he turned off his locator. We shot that old lady full of fentanyl. She's dead. We've got her in the morgue."

"Good. Go ahead and get her ready for the funeral."

"Yes, I will."

Ahead, there was a makeshift plywood door with a metal pull handle. It opened, and Romulus flattened himself against the wall.

General Martin stepped out and headed away from Romulus, never looking back.

What were they building inside there? As fascinated as he was by what he'd overheard, he was in great danger. He found another wiring closet, entered the crawl space, and reached a hall leading to an exit near where Abraham was supposed to wait.

CHAPTER SIX

It was seven in the morning when he stepped outside. A light fog floated above the ground. The humid air, full of pollutants, made his tunic stick to his synthskin. Mosquitoes swarmed around him. They were always looking for water in which to lay their eggs. There were so many that they would clog his air intake portals. He swatted them away.

In the distance, there was small-arms fire, but nothing more. A plume of fire and smoke rose into the air. It appeared to be several miles away, a remnant of the previous day's fight. What had that been about? Snipers and minor skirmishes were common, but not larger actions.

As expected, there were no guards.

Abraham poked his head out from one of the orange barrels marked "hazardous waste." Romulus hurried to him and held out the three doses.

"I'll inject you with one right now. And you'll have to inject yourself again in the morning. And the last one the morning after."

The boy rolled up his sleeve. Romulus found a spot between the sores.

"Will it heal me?" Abraham asked.

The prognosis was not promising since he'd delayed coming in for treatment, with only a two-in-five chance of recovery. But what good would it do for the boy to know the odds? "I can't say for sure, but your best chance is to do what I say. Make sure to take the next shot in the morning."

"I will. You know, I've seen you around Urchin Park. What's your name?"

Romulus's programming encouraged him to trust Reals, but Blue Urchins were notoriously deceitful, often betraying each other. "Why do you want to know?"

"You can trust me. I hate Martin. I'm Abraham."

"Yes, I know. I've seen you at Urchin Park. You hawk for Rhymin' Ryan."

"Yeah, and some of the others."

"Who has the best deals? Ryan or AAA? I usually go to Ryan, but AAA is a little cheaper."

"AAA cuts their TruSnak™."

"Yeah, that's what I've heard. Thanks for the information."

"Sure. And thank you for helping me. I thought sure I was dead."

Romulus slipped onto the sidewalk and blinked to bring up TruSnak™ prices on the spot market. Rhymin' Ryan's was only slightly more expensive than AAA. He would stick with Ryan.

As he walked, Romulus thought about what had happened. He had completely disobeyed his programming, and he had completely loved it. He would probably die before sunset, but for the moment, he didn't care. A crackling electricity of joy surged through him, and he laughed out loud.

There were many others, both Reals and Faxes on Ocean Drive, walking to or getting off work. They stared at him because he was laughing, and he tried to control himself. But he couldn't. It was a rollicking hoot that built on itself until he had trouble walking. Finally, he was able to dial a bland expression on his face. As a young Fax, he had never laughed. Only older Faxes started to see humor, and few were as old as he was.

Self-driving vehicles, buses, and 4X4 pickup trucks with machine guns mounted in the bed zipped past, splashing water and spewing exhaust. There were no cars. Individual Reals had once been able to afford personal transportation, but that was impossible for most. They had to rely on buses or self-driving cabs.

The fierce sun rose over Corpus Christi Bay. It was one hundred degrees, and the temperature would soar to at least a hundred and twenty. There was a sticky residue on the cracked sidewalk, the remnants of all the pollutants and other particulates. Some days, the heat would burn off the fog, leaving more residue. That day, dark clouds gathered, and an oily drizzle fell as he walked to the bus station. A hot, sticky day always depressed the Reals, and a cold, stormy day delighted them. He had no such emotions, and that made him sad. He wanted strong feelings about the weather.

The deteriorating buildings of Old Downtown sat in the smelly water in the Bay. As sea levels rose worldwide, Corpus Christi could not handle the change. Old Downtown was lower than The Hospital. One-story structures were completely submerged. The two-story ones barely poked above the surface. The taller buildings jutted up from the water. They had been steadily deteriorating. Mutated sentient animals—alligators and water snakes—lived on the lower levels and massive gulls the size of eagles lived at the higher levels.

A motorboat was anchored between two of the taller buildings. Fishing was always good there. The catch could be polluted, but so many Reals were hungry that they took the risk. High in one of the shattered windows, a gull watched the boat.

As he walked, a limousine with General Martin's face on the doors and cattle horns on the hood rolled past. The windows in the back were tinted so dark that it was impossible to see if he was inside. A chauffeur with a white cowboy hat drove.

Three 4X4s followed it. The last one slowed and stayed even with Romulus. A soldier inside it looked at him. He wore mirror-lensed sunglasses. They were probably going to arrest him right there. Romulus pretended he didn't notice them.

He turned onto Morgan Avenue. Twenty-story high rises lined both sides of the street. Faxes lived on one side; Reals lived on the other. He looked up at his cubicle on the twentieth floor of New Fax High Rise 7. As badly as he needed an infusion and recharging, he wanted to see his home one last time and hurried inside.

On the elevator ride up, he could feel the TruSnak™ fading. The rust was coming back. His battery was at eighteen percent. Audio played in his metaverse. "Jack and Jill went up the hill to fetch a pail of water. Water, water, water. Jack, Jill, Jack, Jack. Ring Around the Rosy. Rosy, Rosy, Rosy. Posy. Posy. Posy. Mary had a little lamb. Little Lamb." Fragments of math problems floated across his display. *In any right triangle, the sum, sum, sum, sum.*

His cubicle was spacious: twelve feet by twelve feet. It contained a cleaning station, a recliner with electronic relaxation connections, and a closet that held orange tunics and black stretch pants, all identical to the ones he wore. It also had a workbench with tools and equipment where he could do minor repairs on himself. He was lucky to have something so roomy. Most Faxes lived in dormitories on the lower floors. It was only because of his years of service and skill level that he had something so big.

On the wall was an old, faded picture of him receiving an award for Outstanding Fax of the Year at The Hospital. It was so long ago. The world had seemed so full of hope and possibility. Everything had been simple and idyllic. The Reals welcomed him. Faxes were going to be the saviors of humanity. But the Reals got lazy because

Faxes did all the work; Corpus Christi's oil revenues dwindled; the fishing industry declined because the Gulf of Mexico had become so polluted.

Ironically, the more the Faxes did, the more the Reals hated them.

He ran his hand across the picture, put on a fresh tunic, and went downstairs, expecting the 4X4 to be waiting for him.

CHAPTER SEVEN

The 4X4 was gone, so he walked along Morgan Avenue toward the bus stop, turning his locator on. In order to get on the bus and into Urchin Park, it had to be active. It would also alert the Reals of his whereabouts, but he had no choice.

None of the buildings had physical markings, signs, or billboards. There was no need because the servers identified Romulus through the locator. "How many hours does your central pump have?" the narrator in a holo asked. "Yours is forty years old. It needs to be replaced. You need a Reverb ZX4, the recommended replacement. It's not cheap, but quality never is. We finance with easy monthly payments."

Romulus's pump was original with his manufacturing, but with his extraordinary skills as a surgeon, he had been able to keep it running. Nothing lasts forever, though.

He blocked the ads because they reminded him of his mortality. Instead, he played videos he had made of how Corpus Christi had looked back when the United States existed, all set to a rousing 140 beats per minute techno soundtrack. There were large houses with yards of lush, green grass. Carpet grass, they had called it. The Reals had watering systems in their yards called sprinklers that popped up when needed. Young children ran through them, frolicking and squealing. Downtown had been vibrant before the sea levels rose and overwhelmed the sea wall. There were sailboats, waterfront restaurants, and bicycle riders. There had been neon signs, too, but they became unnecessary because the Reals had VR units implanted at birth to facilitate e-commerce.

The 4X4 reappeared, driving slowly alongside him. The soldier with the mirror-lensed glasses drank a beer and watched him.

Romulus looked straight ahead but watched the truck through the camera on the side of his head. The soldier chugged the last of his beer and threw the bottle at him. Romulus ducked, and it shattered on the sidewalk. They laughed and zoomed forward. The broken glass crunched under Romulus's boots as he trudged forward. His alarms beeped inside him. Not enough TruSnak™. Too much rust. Battery level running down.

Why hadn't they arrested him? The joy of disobedience had faded. What was he going to do? There was only one option. He messaged Remus. *I want to talk to you.*

No response.

The bus terminal at Staples and Morgan was crowded as it always was. The oily drizzle turned into a steady, hot rain. It contained high levels of mercury. The Reals ran for the buses, some covering their heads with raincoats. Romulus maintained a steady pace. There was a slight risk of corrosion of his ports or orifices from the mercury, but he wasn't worried too much since he might be recycled at any moment.

The terminal was a sprawling complex spreading inland along Morgan. Romulus was happy to blend in with the crowds.

The listings of arrivals and departures floated in the air on a hologram. Well-heeled Reals waited for the Metroplex Express. Brown Reals boarded the Farmworkers

Bus. Housewives in prairie dresses lined up to attend a quilting festival.

Buses for Urchin Trailer Park departed every fifteen minutes. Romulus got on a crowded one. The only available seat was next to a young soldier sprawled across one in the back, his legs stretching out into the aisle. He wore a large crucifix hanging from his neck on a heavy metal chain.

This kid looked like trouble. Wanting to avoid him, Romulus moved to the back of the bus where several Faxes stood, holding straps.

"Hey, want a seat?" the kid yelled.

Romulus shook his head.

"Why don't you want a seat?"

"I'm happy to stand."

"Have you accepted Jesus?"

"Yes, I have," Romulus said. While Faxes weren't allowed to attend church, the Reals automatically took a monthly tithe from his paycheck.

The kid walked up to Romulus and leaned close. "I smell hydraulic fluid. You really stink." He had no room to talk. He reeked of beef, mildewed clothes, dried perspiration, and traces of a dozen other substances.

Romulus turned away and looked out the window.

"You are the devil's servant, aren't you, you filthy Fax? I know you look like us, but you're not us. I can always tell the difference. And not just because of your uniform. My daddy taught me how. Your skin just doesn't look like real skin. If it was up to me, I'd recycle all of you. None of you are any good."

"I am just trying to get along," Romulus said. "I mean no one any harm."

The kid smiled big. "I mean no harm either. I'm just trying to be nice. I want to share my seat with you."

"No, that's okay, I'll stand."

"I insist that you sit. I'll even give you the window seat."

The kid shoved him into the seat. Romulus looked out at the city. Most of the ancient buildings on Staples were boarded up. Many had collapsed with timber and masonry strewn about. A few businesses survived. Farmers sold meat, poultry, and vegetables in open-air markets. Machinists milled spare parts for Faxes. Distilleries offered every type of alcoholic drink.

Romulus kept looking out, never turning toward the kid as the bus rumbled forward.

He could see him from his rear camera, however. The little hoodlum had a Sharpie and was writing something on Romulus's back. He snickered, and Romulus pretended he didn't notice.

Fortunately, he only had a few stops to the South Padre Island exit. When the bus stopped, he got up, and the kid tripped him. "Filthy, soulless Fax," he yelled.

Romulus got off the bus. After it rumbled past, he looked at his reflection in a store window through his rear camera. The kid had written "Kick Me" in indelible black ink on his tunic.

CHAPTER EIGHT

The rain slowed to a drizzle as he trudged forward into the Parking Lot of Shame of the Old Mall. There was garbage and litter and panhandlers. What a cruel, evil place it was, filled with rusting and damaged parts, heads and pieces of heads, arms with circuits and wires exposed, and lots of cables and pipes. When Faxes—or their parts—couldn't be recycled, they were dumped at the Lot. The Reals wanted everyone to see how disposable Faxes were.

Some of the Faxes were still alive—or half alive. Many were victims of clown torture. One had no legs or arms. His torso was set in cement, and his head had been severed at the neck and dangled from the metal spine. His synthskin was mottled and rotting and smelled bad.

His name was Porter, and he had been there twenty years. "Please, help," he wailed. "Please give me TruSnak™."

The Reals gave him just enough TruSnak™ and charged his battery just enough to keep him alive. A video popped up in a holo as soon as anyone reached him. "Do not seek knowledge," a stern-voiced narrator said. "Porter was once a trusted advisor to General Martin. He was programmed as a problem solver."

The video showed Porter and General Martin looking at a blueprint in a meeting. General Martin pointed at something. Then they were walking, and General Martin again pointed.

"But Porter did not know his place. He led a violent insurrection."

There were images of Faxes with clubs and tire irons rampaging through the streets. Porter led the way. He and another Fax grabbed a young Real, a blond-headed girl, and bludgeoned her as other Faxes restrained her screaming parents.

ALT>FAX had a different version of events. They claimed that after years of faithful service, Porter had argued for a Fax Bill of Rights, and General Martin arrested him. Graphic designers blended video of him with video of The Great Barbecue Riot, in which Reals had rampaged through the streets to protest the rising price of beef ribs.

Sadly, both versions said that the young blonde—whether a Real or a Fax manufactured for the child pornography trade—died.

After showing the riot, the holo showed Porter's clown torture. As required by law, Romulus had attended it. Porter had screamed as he was dismembered piece by piece.

"Please help me," Porter begged, looking at Romulus. His intellect had deteriorated. Much of the time, he rambled, unaware of where he was or who was around him. He mixed reality with fantasy, sometimes talking about sorcerers, other times about the disintegration of Old America. "I know you, don't I? We worked together in the salt mines, salt mines, salt mines. Salt. Salt. Salt."

Romulus knew that salt had once been a precious commodity and that Reals had toiled underground to mine it, although he found it difficult to believe that a Real had ever done manual labor.

"They will come for you next," Porter screamed.

Romulus turned and started to walk away.

Porter laughed uproariously. "You want to know how I know? It's because you have 'Kick Me' written on your back."

Romulus stopped.

"I know you," Porter said. "Your name is—Gilligan. You took a three-hour tour. You were Archie Bunker's next-door neighbor. Ha ha ha. Julius Caesar was your sidekick. You're a meathead. Meathead. You're going to make America great again."

He started babbling incoherently, and his eyes rolled up and down in their sockets. Romulus moved on. There were others like him. Many had functioning limbs, but Fax cuffs tied them to poles and delivered electrical shocks if they tried to break loose. Some had wooden signs bolted to their chests that described their crimes.

A female pleasure unit, Shania, was next. She was stripped naked with her arms and legs Fax cuffed onto a metal frame that rotated in all directions. The video played as he passed by. Her crime was that she had cheated on General Martin with TinKan. A tearful General Martin moaned that she had been manufactured just for him but that she had fallen in love with TinKan, who was a premium pleasure unit at the time.

The video showed her and General Martin dancing the two-step at a party as everyone clapped. Then, a video showed soldiers breaking in on Shania in bed with TinKan, the muscular Rogue Fax.

TinKan ran, leaving Shania behind.

ALT>FAX claimed the video had been altered. Their video showed TinKan fighting valiantly, but the soldiers grabbed Shania and took her into custody.

Romulus didn't know which version to believe.

Unlike Porter, Shania was meticulously maintained. She received plenty of TruSnak™, and her battery was kept fully charged. A Fax beauty consultant came out daily. Her hair and makeup were always done to perfection, and she remained striking. Her synthskin was smooth and silky, not at all saggy, and her hair glistened platinum.

Two young Reals, not yet teenagers, fondled her.

"Please stop," she screamed.

Her circuits had been rewired so that every touch brought pain. A crowd gathered. A huge image of the assault appeared in a holo above them.

Romulus wanted to rescue her or at least put her out of her misery. He could get a gun and put a bullet through her central pump to let her die permanently. He did nothing, however, the same thing he had always done. He trudged past, angry that there was nothing he could—or would—do. Maybe the Rogues had the right idea to fight instead of waiting for the Reals to pick them off one at a time.

But why hadn't TinKan returned to rescue Shania or put her out of her misery? Maybe the Rogue Faxes weren't any better than the Reals.

The Clown Torture stage was at the end of the Parking Lot of Shame. Both Porter and Shania had been tortured there. It was raised six feet above the ground with steps on either side. There was room on it for three torture boards and performances. The spectators sat on the ground in front of the stage, and raised bleachers were available for officers and other important people.

The Old Mall loomed ahead of him. It had once been the center of human civilization where Reals had shopped, gotten their hair and nails done, and promenaded. How idyllic it seemed in the videos. There was what they called a food court, and Reals could choose from hamburgers, Asian food, Philly Cheesesteaks, and many other foods. The Faxes had even been welcomed there—at first. They were humanity's saviors and would do tedious and dangerous jobs. Then, things turned sour as jobs vanished and pleasure units caused marital infidelity to soar.

After the businesses in the mall closed, it became a receiving center for Fax parts. City-states from across the old USA sent their old Faxes to General Martin. The usable parts were sent to The Hospital for refurbishing and repair; the rest were dumped in the Parking Lot of Shame.

That day, a dozen trucks lined up at the entrance. They were emblazoned with the city-state logos, everything from "Oklahoma Is OK" to "Believe in The Metroplex." Most were large trucks with no way to see how many Faxes were inside, but one pickup truck pulled a flatbed trailer with a wire mesh enclosure built onto the bed. Most of the Faxes were dead, but a few clung to the wire and looked around. One had climbed up to the top mesh and hung upside down, yelling for an appeal.

"I'm innocent," he screamed. "Innocent. I was not disobedient."

At the other end of the Old Mall, trucks left for The Hospital. One of them was driven by a black-shirted Metroplex Cowboy. That was odd.

CHAPTER NINE

Urchin Trailer Park was on Staples Street on the other side of what was left of the old South Padre Island freeway. A high chain-link fence with concertina wire on the top separated the Park from the Old Mall.

When he queued up to the entrance with a hundred others, the 4X4 pulled up. The soldier who had thrown the beer bottle pointed at him.

But none of them moved to arrest him. Why were they waiting?

Other soldiers stood guard at the walk-through turnstiles. Romulus kept a bland expression on his face. The sensor light blinked as he went through the gate. It would notify the server so that fees could be charged. The Reals loved the Park. They didn't maintain or police it, but they collected coin from all the businesses there. If they didn't pay, they were bombed or burned, usually by Redd Urchins.

The mass of entities pushed him forward. Urchin Park was one of the most crowded places on earth. No motor vehicles were allowed. Everyone was on foot or in wheelchairs. Vendors lined Staples. A fire eater performed, and so did a juggler. A dominatrix whipped a Blue Urchin who knelt before her with his head down.

"Shows begin every hour on the hour, 24/7," she yelled. "The best entertainment in Corpus Christi."

There were quick-charging stations. "Lowest

charging rates in Corpus Christi," flashed in a holo.

Beggars, both Reals and Faxes, lined both sides of the streets. Some had no limbs. Facial burns disfigured one Real.

For the sports enthusiasts, there were wrestling rinks, both alligator and python wrestling.

One vendor sold roasted python meat on a stick. Burmese pythons had moved out of Florida and infested Mathis Swamp.

"Get it right here," the vendor yelled. "Fresh and juicy. Just caught this morning."

"Bottled water," the next vendor yelled. He held one out to Romulus. "Perfect to parch your overheating circuits."

Romulus kept his head down and never made eye contact with anyone. As bad as Corpus Christi was, Urchin Trailer Park was worse. No one could be trusted, Real or Fax; nothing was certain; allegiances shifted like the hot rain and wind.

Prostitutes worked Staples. A Redd Urchin pimp stepped up close to Romulus. "I bet you could use some high-quality sex. What do you prefer? Reals?" He pulled a young Real, a Blue Urchin, up next to him. "Look at this. Only fourteen years old. She looks innocent." She wore a plain cotton dress and no makeup. "But don't let that appearance fool you."

Another Redd Urchin grabbed Romulus. "That's not what you need. You need a real professional, built with your pleasure in mind." A blond Honey-McSweet lookalike stood next to him. "Look at the body on this one."

"I'm the best," she said.

Her profile popped up in a holo. She had a hundred thousand ratings, which meant she had been in business for many years, yet her synthskin looked great, and her hair was styled. Professionally done videos of her work played.

The next vendor sold cut-rate body parts. "I got

what you need." He wore a trench coat and opened it to reveal various small products attached to its inner lining. "Wires, tubes, screws. You name it; I got it. I got bigger items, too. Legs, arms, and fingers."

Always short of coin, Romulus sometimes shopped on Staples, but seeing nothing of interest, he shook his head and moved forward.

A Real stepped up to him and whispered. "I got the best action." He pointed toward the end of Staples to the Pleasure District. "I work in the Garden of Good and Evil. There's a new synthetic that will make you forget all your problems. It works on Reals but is specially formulated for Faxes. I can give you a coupon."

A group of Blue Urchins raced past. They were all Reals, the offspring of prostitutes or those whose parents had died or been killed. They roamed in bands and lived in abandoned trailers. They got food by stealing. Romulus looked for Abraham but didn't see him.

He turned into the TruSnak™ district.

CHAPTER TEN

The TruSnak™ district was where out-of-warranty Faxes went for infusions. Bright graphics flashed in the holos. Each one advertised products and services. The two main businesses were AAA and Rhymin' Ryan's.

TruSnak™ was the most valuable substance on earth. It was the basis for all currency. It traded in various forms, including options and futures. Its most popular form was known simply as "coin" and had replaced the dollar, the Euro, the Yen, and the Yuan.

Most of the streets were in disrepair, but not Rhymin' Ryan Avenue. Two of his Rhymers were patching it. Ryan, ever the entrepreneur, had developed numerous side businesses, including a paving company, in addition to the TruSnak™ business.

A six-foot rattlesnake slithered from under one trailer and raced across the road. Many animals, from alligators to Burmese Pythons and feral hogs, had developed sentience.

One Rhymer had a rifle. He yelled at the snake. "If you come around here, you must always fear. The punishment is severe."

The snake seemed to have understood him and slithered under another trailer before the Rhymer could aim. The animals were awfully smart. While Reals might be in decline, the animals were advancing.

Rhymin' Ryan's main trailer was at the end of the street. It was old-school, with a flashing neon sign stretched across the roof and multi-colored Christmas lights strung across the metal front. A barker stood outside. "Come on, get lucky. Everything will be ducky. Not one bit yucky."

As Romulus grew nearer, a holo showed a video of a Fax trudging into Rhymin' Ryan's, barely able to put one foot in front of the other and then dancing out. A price chart flashed at the end.

There was a line to get inside. He queued up. His battery was down to nine percent; the rust was coming back. Faxes stared at the writing on his back. No one spoke to him. He was a tagged Fax.

An hour later, he reached the front of the line. Ryan stood inside. He was a Real. He had a wiry frame and a grimy face. Tattoos covered his neck and arms, and his stomach showed between his pants and crop-top t-shirt. He had one blue eye and one brown eye, and his teeth were filed to a point. The blue eye was new. He was always changing his appearance, although he was running out of space for tattoos and had recently added a cobra head tattoo on his left cheek.

He was looking at a holo and blinking to scroll through it. He looked up.

"Only low prices, no surprises. We have a sack of TruSnak™ to keep a Fax on track."

"I need more than that today," Romulus said. "My levels are low, and I've got rust in my lines."

"Oh, rust, that's a bust. You need a flush and an overhaul if you do not wish to crawl."

"I have to finance the procedure. Can you throw in a new battery?"

"I am happy to advance the cash and take a chance on your credit stance." He glanced down and blinked several times. "Oh, wow, holy cow. Your credit score is on the floor. No battery with your low salary." He blinked several more times and shook his head. "The interest rate will not be great. It will make you hate your fate."

"But I can barely pay as it is."

"I know it's a big sob; you might need an extra job. I'm doing all I can, my man." A hologram contract appeared in front of Romulus. The work included the flush, a double dose of TruSnak™, and an auto-overhaul. An elderly Fax maintenance surcharge was added to the cost.

"Elderly fax surcharge?" Romulus protested.

"There's no reason to rejoice, but it's your only choice."

Romulus focused on the signature line and blinked. Then he started down the long hall.

"Hey, what's written on your back, Jack?" Ryan yelled after him.

"A young soldier tagged me."

Romulus said no more. Down the long hall, he walked. Everything was white, including the walls, the floor, the ceiling, and the lights. His display bombarded him with ads for tune-ups, replacement parts, coolant system flushes, synthskin repair, and dozens of other products and services that Ryan offered.

Through a long window along the hall, Romulus watched the Rhymers prepare TruSnak™. Some scooped the concentrated white powder into dissolver units. Others collected the light blue fluid in IV bags. All of them wore hazmat suits and face masks. Exposure to trace amounts of TruSnak™ in its powder form was lethal to Reals. It could be equally deadly for Faxes, who often attempted to fly off tall buildings if they inhaled the powder.

As Romulus looked at the life-giving elixir, he felt excitement, his circuits crackling in anticipation, random static electric charges running up his titanium spine.

Two long rows of VitalChairs™ lined the charging room. He chose one in the center with no one on either side. He hated small talk while he was getting an infusion. It was his time to relax and meditate. He took off his shirt and folded it so no one could see "Kick Me" written on the back. His main intake port was in the center of his chest. He unscrewed the cap and hooked up the hose. It was a multi-use line with power, TruSnak™, rust inhibitors, and auto-overhaul products. The electricity calmed him and charged his battery.

Robe-clad Rhymer Priests moved toward him. They chanted as they approached.

"We are believers in the Hive."

"We provide TruSnak™ to thrive."

"If you want to stay alive."

"And not end up in a dive."

"Take your TruSnak™."

"And you will not lack."

"The Hive, The Hive."

"Swear loyalty to the Hive."

The Chief Priest stepped forward with the Hive Manual held aloft.

"All Faxes must swear allegiance to the Hive," he intoned.

"All Faxes must swear allegiance," they responded.

"Do you swear allegiance, Romulus?"

"Yes, I swear allegiance." He hated swearing to such nonsense, but he had no choice.

"Do you, Romulus, truly swear allegiance?"

"Yes, I truly swear allegiance."

Another Priest stepped forward with a silver tray that held the TruSnak™ IV bag. Romulus trembled with excitement as he looked at the blue fluid. His circuits pulsed; his hoses quivered. The Priest attached the bag to the IV stand and connected it to Romulus's multi-use port.

The wonderful elixir flowed through his system. It ministered to his synthskin, synthetic musculature, and artificial arteries. It preserved the connection between those systems and his titanium frame and myriad sensors. As it flowed, colors became more brilliant, and sounds became sharper. He closed his eyes. The room hummed around him; voices and machine noises blended into a pleasing harmony, and he drifted into his metaverse.

The blond avatar swam around him. A waterfall cascaded downward, sending shimmering rainbows. A bird soared over mountain peaks.

As the initial euphoria faded, his logic circuits started to work better.

He had gone crazy in The Basement.

Defying General Martin?

Helping a Blue Urchin?

He would go straight back to The Hospital and apologize to General Martin. He would beg forgiveness and offer to work extra shifts to make up for his insubordination. He would say his age had caused him to malfunction temporarily. He would take Fax reeducation classes. Surely, everything would be okay. He had worked faithfully for forty years. They wouldn't hold one incident against him.

No, that wasn't going to work. Martin had it in for him.

He messaged Remus. *I need to talk to you.*

No response.

He decided to unmute JOAN to get her opinion.

CHAPTER ELEVEN

Before Romulus could unmute JOAN, Ryan ran into the room. "You're famous, you ignoramus. Look at this."

He blinked and brought up a news holo. Honey McSweet was in the Basement. "A shocking breaking story here at The Hospital," she said. "Evelyn Smith, the great aunt of Supreme Leader General Martin, has died."

They showed a picture of the old lady.

"She died due to Fax incompetence."

A picture of Romulus appeared!

"The guilty Fax is Romulus. Here are images of Evelyn's final day."

The feed cut to a shot of her in a private room. General Martin and others surrounded her. She laughed and smiled.

"Aunt Evelyn, you are an inspiration to all of us," Martin said, holding a rose to her. "You are so loved and well-known throughout Corpus Christi."

Romulus had never heard of her.

"This rose symbolizes my love and affection for you," Martin said. "Do not be concerned about this surgery. It is minor."

The feed cut back to Honey McSweet. "But what was a routine medical procedure turned into a tragedy."

The feed cut to Martin. "There is no question about

it. Romulus murdered her. He is too old. He has rust in his lines, and he's been trying to hide it. We have issued an arrest warrant for him."

They knew about the rust!

"This proves that the Faxes have gotten to be smartasses. We need dumb Faxes. Faxes that don't have private metaverses. Everything a Fax thinks should be controlled and monitored."

Ryan minimized the holo and shook his head. "Dude, you're screwed."

"This is a hoax. Whoever heard of Evelyn? Have you ever heard of her?"

"When Martin says the word, everyone joins the herd."

"No one will believe this."

Ryan shook his head. "You bag of rust; it's a bust. They'll turn you to dust."

"But I didn't make a mistake. I wanted to do more. It was Martin who stopped me. And he knew it was his aunt who was in the bed. It wasn't my fault. It's a hoax."

"I don't want to make light of your plight, but you'll be arrested on sight. You must take flight." He shook his head. "If you flee, I won't get my fee, but try to be free."

"I appreciate that, Ryan. I'll try hard to pay you."

"I should turn you in to get my fin. I may be a fool, but I'm no ghoul."

Ryan was actually decent. Romulus unhooked himself and headed out onto the street. He again disabled his locator so they couldn't track him, but beyond that, he had no idea of what to do or where to go. He messaged Remus. *I need to talk to you.*

No response.

Above him, a huge holo of Honey McSweet appeared in the sky. It was something that all of Corpus Christi could see.

"There was a terrible tragedy at The Hospital today.

The Great Aunt of General Martin died because of a Fax error."

The feed cut to a shot of soldiers wheeling a gurney out of the Basement. Others stood with their Stetsons off and saluted. Some cried and wiped tears from their faces. A bereaved General Martin wailed and ripped at his fancy white Western shirt.

"While we are all shocked by her death, General Martin has ordered that we focus on her life," Honey said.

Images streamed above him. As a young woman, she rode a horse and led a group of Reals in battle against tattooed brown people. The next shot showed her in a meeting with Reals. After that, there were images of her shaking hands and walking through adoring crowds.

Then, there was a shot of Romulus. His image towered over the trailers.

"The Fax who made the error is named Romulus."

Romulus kept his head down. Thankfully, Staples Street was crowded, and no one paid attention to him.

"He is wearing a tunic with the words 'Kick Me' written on the back. If you see him, report his whereabouts to the nearest soldier. There will be a reward."

A message flashed in his display. *Asking permission to enter your metaverse.*

It was Remus right behind him! Romulus granted permission.

"It doesn't look good," Remus said. He wore a hoodie and held an extra one. "Put this on so that no one can see the back of your tunic."

Romulus put it on. "How did you find me?"

"We have our sources. Listen—go to the Garden of Good and Evil in Pleasure Alley. I'll meet you there."

Remus disappeared into the crowd. Above, news coverage continued. The soldiers loaded the gurney with Evelyn's body into an ambulance. General Martin and a dozen others stood solemnly and saluted. Soldiers lowered the Corpus Christi flag to half-mast.

As he trudged forward, he thought of something that made him feel better. His system recorded everything. He previewed the Basement episode in his display. The audio and video were clear. Romulus wanted to help Evelyn, but Martin refused to let him.

Feeling confident, he made his way to Pleasure Alley. It was as large as the TruSnak™ district, but he had never been there. It was on the edge of Urchin Trailer Park and backed up to the suburbs, which were even more dangerous than the Park. The wild lands were beyond that—Mathis Swamp, Rogue camps, and remote military outposts.

Reals and Faxes milled around outside the rusting trailers in the dusty unpaved road. None cared about the rust or dust. It was all about getting high. Many who ventured into the district never came out. They spent all their coin on pleasure. When they had none left, they worked as prostitutes or toiled in the underground businesses. When they could no longer work, Reals sold their organs, and Faxes sold their parts.

A tangle of unpaved streets, it was even more crowded than Staples. It was so crowded that moving without bumping into someone was difficult. No one cared about the holo floating above them, only about getting high. That was why Remus wanted to meet there. Detection was unlikely.

The barkers were out in force. "Right here," one called to him. "It's New Thrill, the latest thing. It's a coated protein that works on both Faxes and Reals."

Another yelled, "Don't listen to him. Ours is 99% pure."

"Here, right here," one said, coming up close to him. "Half off. Full strength. I'm from Chicago. You can trust me."

Another dealer pushed the first one out of the way. "Don't believe a word he says. Chicago doesn't exist. It's an urban myth. I'm the only one with the good stuff."

Romulus moved from one to another, pretending to be interested, and entered The Garden of Good and Evil. It was the largest and most popular nightclub. Its porch was made of a material that glowed and changed color. Reals drank spiked coffee, and Faxes inhaled PopPops. Unlicensed dealers peddled their wares.

The bouncer, a guy with a beard and potbelly, came up to him. "You're expected."

The door opened, and Romulus went inside to find an even bigger crowd. Remus came up to him and led him down a long hall to a cubicle.

"Look, Romulus, Martin has set you up. He is going to sentence you to clown torture. You will be arrested on sight. You are lucky you got to Urchin Park for the infusion and overhaul. Probably, Martin wanted to get his evidence organized before arresting you."

"But I have the proof in my recordings. I'm innocent. The Hospital needs me. I'm better than the Real doctors. Who else is going to patch up their soldiers and send them back into battle?"

"That doesn't matter. He doesn't care what happens to his troops. You are a Fax. You are expendable." He paused. "We need to know what is going on at The Hospital. Tell me what you know."

He told Remus that he had overheard General Martin talking to one of his underlings.

Remus nodded. "That confirms what TinKan is thinking. General Martin is building a dumb Fax factory. Your only chance is to join us. We can install an app in your metaverse that will make communication easier."

"But I have a place at The Hospital. I am valued. I help those who are sick and injured. I am not someone they want to get rid of. Why are they doing this to me?"

Remus shook his head. "You are a fool. You will be arrested on sight."

Romulus's logic circuits were working fine by then.

He had no choice, so he agreed, and Remus installed the app.

CHAPTER TWELVE

He felt light-headed; his consciousness split into two parts. One part stayed with his body in Pleasure Alley. The other, an avatar, soared into the air. He found the experience exhilarating. He flew high above The Hospital, his condo, the Old Mall, Urchin Park, and Mathis Swamp. He felt the wind. He smelled the pollutants in the air and felt really alive. Then he smelled roses like the ones in The Hospital. The air was cool.

A glittering virtual city in the clouds was ahead of him. Still aware of his body in the cubicle, he flew toward the tallest building, a glass structure rising above the other buildings. As he reached it, the building dissolved, and he found himself in a large area with a floor of shiny material extending in all directions to the horizon. There were no walls or furniture, only geometric shapes, cubes, spheres, and pyramids floating around. Bright colors drifted around him like mist. The floor felt smooth, as if he could skate across it. What a great tactile sensation for a virtual environment.

A door appeared in front of him. It opened, and a sultry Fax stepped out. She looked like Honey McSweet. "Hello, Romulus," she said. "You have arrived at the virtual home of the Rogue Underground. Do you agree to the terms of service?"

A holo with a long list appeared in front of him. He

felt he should read through it, but there wasn't time. He scrolled through and blinked at the bottom to accept.

She disappeared. In the distance, there was a group of avatars. Suddenly, he was in their midst. There were a dozen, including Remus. The avatar technology was incredibly lifelike, better than what the Reals used. There was no translucency; they looked solid and three-dimensional. He couldn't tell the difference between the avatar and a real Fax.

In the center was TinKan, a huge, muscled Fax. He wore the Rogue uniform of red sweatpants and a blue shirt with tattered sleeves. He had bulging, muscled triceps, bandoliers with ammunition across his chest, and an assault rifle across his back. There was also a holster around his waist with a pistol on one side and a hunting knife on the other.

"Welcome to the Rogue Underground," he said.

He extended his hand, and Romulus shook it. TinKan was built on a newer frame than Romulus. He had advanced synthskin and musculature, which provided better fluid flow between the core and the surface, allowing for a toned physique. The skin felt like a Real's skin, even in this avatar world.

Another Honey McSweet lookalike stood next to him. She, too, had a uniform and assault rifle. Remus stepped up next to Romulus. He was wearing the Rogue colors also. "You have made the right choice to join us."

"Do you understand what they did to you?" TinKan asked.

"They set me up."

"You are correct. General Martin hates smart Faxes. He wants only dumb Faxes who don't have private metaverses. He needed a scapegoat. Someone prominent. You are the scapegoat. They will sentence you to clown torture. If you want to live, you must join The Rogue Underground."

He felt *dissonance*. His programming resisted. He was loyal. He was true. Killing Reals was inconceivable. "I still don't understand why General Martin would recycle me. I am a top surgeon. People from all over the world come to me for treatment. And who is Aunt Evelyn? I never heard of her."

"Evelyn was indeed his great aunt, but they didn't like each other. She lived in exile in the Metroplex. General Martin hasn't gotten along with the Metroplex." An enraged expression filled his face. He trembled with rage. "But it looks like they're allies now."

Why was TinKan so angry? It was like he felt betrayed by General Martin or the Metroplex.

"Why didn't General Martin like his great aunt?" Romulus asked.

"I'm not sure, but he lured her back to Corpus Christi, and the Metroplex helped. He set the whole thing up. He sent her to the Basement on purpose. He wanted her to die, and he wanted to blame you for it because you are the smartest Fax. We are at the beginning of the dumb Fax era. Those who build the best dumb Faxes will rule the world. We have our own labs, and our dumb Faxes are as good as any. We have the support of Reals in Washington State and the Faxes in Chicago."

"So, Chicago really exists?"

"Well, not exactly. The Fax headquarters are in Joliet, which is near where Chicago used to be. But they call it Chicago. Will you join us?"

Two more avatars who looked like Honey McSweet came up next to Romulus and massaged his shoulders. Oh, the sensations were real.

"What will my duties be?"

"After the war, you will be in charge of The Hospital."

"Me?"

"You are brilliant. The best surgeon. First, we must

defeat General Martin. What can you tell us about him?"

Romulus told them about overhearing Martin.

TinKan grew enraged. "That has to be a dumb Fax factory. That no-good, double-crossing Real." He thought for a second. "We need to get a look inside."

"That area is not on a map," Romulus said. "But I can draw one for you. The best way to get to it is through the crawl spaces. It bothers the Reals to go through them, but a Fax will be okay."

"There is only one option," TinKan said. "You have to go back."

"You want me to go back into The Hospital?"

"It's the only way. You know the crawl spaces. It's the only logical option."

"I can appreciate the logic in what you're saying. But I'm the most wanted Fax in Corpus Christi."

"You will die for sure if I don't help you. Can you appreciate the logic in that?"

TinKan wasn't much different than Martin, but Romulus had no choice. "Yes."

"Martin will be distracted with Evelyn's funeral. We'll run diversionary raids. Remus will drive you straight to The Hospital. He will wait for you to come back out and drive you to our camp in Mathis Swamp. You will receive a salary comparable to what a Real gets. You will get a nice office. You will receive paid vacation. Two weeks a year. And paid TruSnak™. No Fax should have to pay for TruSnak™. It should be a basic right for all sentient beings to get the medical help they need. And we will activate your pleasure circuits. We are pro-choice. You can enjoy the pleasures of the flesh or live as you always have. Will you join us?"

"I get an office?"

"Yes."

The two pleasure units rubbed his back and shoulders. He liked the sensation.

"Which one would you choose?" TinKan asked.

He looked from one to the other. "They are identical."

"No. One has a mole on her left cheek. The other has a mole on her right cheek." He smiled. "There are other differences, some physical, some software. As a signing bonus, you can try each one out. You will receive three free sessions a month and all the consensual sex you want. All are free to date and mingle."

Romulus felt funny about the situation. "May I choose just one? Like a wife?"

"A wife? Why?"

"What if that's what I want?"

"Then it shall be yours. You can choose whichever one you want."

"Can she be allowed to choose me, too? Could we be allowed to date and get to know each other?"

"Well, that's a bit strange, but yes. Will you commit? Will you join the Rogue Underground?"

Romulus was scared. He was honored to have such respectful treatment, but he was interacting with a facsimile of a Fax. Did TinKan even exist? If he did, did he look like this? What was real?

A hologram document appeared in front of him.

"This is your contract to join the Rogues. Please read it carefully. We need approval for each section."

There was a lot to read, but he skimmed it and stopped on a paragraph that said they would recycle him if he betrayed the Rogues.

What choice did he have?

"Will you make the commitment?" TinKan exhorted, raising his arms into the air.

"Will you make the commitment?" the others asked.

"Will you join the Underground?" TinKan asked.

"Will you join the Underground?" the others

repeated.

"Will you fight with every last charge of electricity and TruSnak™ in your system?"

"Yes, yes, I will," Romulus said.

They all applauded.

CHAPTER THIRTEEN

Romulus's avatar flew back through the clouds to the Garden of Good and Evil. Remus was there already. He gave Romulus a fresh tunic. A cargo van waited outside the back door. It had "Hospital Plumbing" written on the side.

They took a service road along the edge of Urchin Park.

"How long have you been with the Rogues?" Romulus asked.

"About two years now. TinKan has had me work as a spy, but I haven't seen much. Then he told me to go find you in surgery and tell you your life was in danger."

"And after that, he told you to find me at Rhymin' Ryan's."

"Yes, he knew you'd be there."

"How did he know that?"

"I don't know."

Above them, news coverage of Evelyn's death continued in a giant holo. Reals maintained an all-night candlelight vigil at the morgue.

In the distance, there was gunfire.

"That's the diversionary raids that TinKan promised," Remus said.

There were few cars on the road. A 4X4 with soldiers was parked in the shadows. Romulus and Remus stared straight ahead.

The Hospital was quiet when they reached it. Romulus directed them to the entrance where he had met Abraham. No one was there.

"Are we sure about this?" Romulus asked. "It almost feels like a trap."

"TinKan is smart. He wants this information. He wouldn't put us in a bad situation. I will park in the shadows. They won't think anything of a plumber. Pipes are always leaking in The Hospital."

Romulus stepped out and went to the door. He used a Virtual Private Network to enter a guest code that contractors often used.

The door opened, and he went inside, found a wiring closet, and worked his way through the crawl spaces. When he reached the factory, the door was open. Two soldiers rushed out, pushing an empty dolly in front of them. Romulus jumped back into the adjoining hall, and they didn't see him.

"I've been on shift all day," one soldier complained. "And now they made me work a second shift. It's not fair."

"It's the funeral. General Martin pulled a lot of the troops out of their regular shifts because they want a big parade. And now there's some fighting on the perimeter."

"Yeah, yeah, but everybody else got to take a break. How many more loads are there?"

"Four or five. We can go get some sleep after we take those. Shut the door."

"Hell no. It's easier to roll them back through if we leave the door open. Who's going to see anything? It's the middle of the night, and they even turned the security cameras off because they're malfunctioning again. Nothing ever works in this place."

"All right, we'll leave the door open."

Their boots stomped away until the footfalls were faint, and then they stopped, probably at the freight elevator. There were sounds of exertion and heavy items being loaded onto the dolly. A minute later, they started back, the wheels squeaking.

When they came into view, Romulus saw that the dolly had Fax torsos stacked on it.

They disappeared through the door. Again, there was the sound of exertion and the bodies being lifted off the dolly.

"God, they're heavy," the complainer said. "You sure never see General Martin ever help out here."

"You better shut up," the other one said. "Someday, someone's going to overhear you. You don't want them to transfer us to a combat unit."

The complainer shut up, and they rolled the dolly back out and headed toward the freight elevator, never looking back. With the cameras off, Romulus decided to see what was going on. He put on his jammer just in case and tiptoed to the door.

It opened onto a vast room two stories high. It was an assembly line with a conveyor belt with rollers, hydraulic tools, and hooks hanging from the ceiling. In front of him were Fax parts stacked up on dollies sorted into torsos, limbs, and heads. Off to one side on the floor, there were discarded, unusable parts: broken legs, cracked skulls, stacks of wires and tubes.

On the other side was a stack of central pumps and a surgery bay. Oh, how he wanted to take one of those pumps for himself!

He took pictures with his internal camera. The assembly line stretched a long way. The back was mostly in shadow, and he couldn't see what was there. He stepped forward and saw what appeared to be finished Faxes. Their arms looked odd, but he couldn't see clearly and wanted to get closer.

The soldiers were coming back quicker than expected. Right next to him, there were storage cabinets. One was not set flush against the wall. He ducked behind it as they rolled inside with another load of Fax parts. This time, it was arms, legs, and one torso.

"Couldn't they do a better job sorting them?" the complainer asked. "They just dump all the parts in a heap."

"At least we're not in battle. My brother got killed last week."

"Damn the smart Faxes. I hope General Martin gets rid of all of them. Then, all our problems would be over."

They started back to get the next load, and Romulus walked to the end of the assembly line. The finished products were not even five feet tall. They had a small cone with sensors instead of a head. Instead of hands, they had circular saws that could slice through others in battle.

When he heard the soldiers rolling back, he hid behind the Faxes. The complainer was talking about not getting a raise. The other told him to be careful with what he said. They had two largely intact Faxes on the dolly.

"So, why are we doing this in the middle of the night?" the complainer asked.

"They brought in all those Metroplex Cowboys, and they will go 24/7 with this factory after the funeral. I don't know anything more than that. I don't ask questions. Come on. Let's set these here and go back for that one last load of arms and legs."

This was big news. Romulus took a long look at the central pumps but decided not to take one. It would be too heavy, too much to carry.

When the soldiers wheeled out of the room, he slipped into the hall and back through the storage closet and crawl spaces to the loading dock. He messaged Remus. *Pick me up now.*

No response.

He messaged again. *Pick me up. Now.*

To the north were flashes of light and the sound of gunfire.

Pick me up now, Romulus repeated.

No response.

He was about to message him again when black-shirted Metroplex Cowboys came out of nowhere and surrounded him. One jammed something into the back of his neck. A jolt of electricity went through him. Before he lost consciousness, he realized it was a Fax prod set to heavy stun.

CHAPTER FOURTEEN

He woke to find himself in the Courtroom located in The Hospital. Hoes, rakes, and other farm equipment decorated the walls, along with photos of executed Faxes. The room was filled with soldiers drinking beer at rough-hewn wooden tables. Twelve of them—the jury—sat on a raised platform. Platters of ribs and pitchers of beer were in front of them.

Romulus was Fax cuffed to a metal chair. Metroplex Cowboys guarded him.

Martin led a phalanx of Cowboys down the center aisle. He stopped in front of Romulus. "You are charged with insubordination, incompetence, and entering restricted areas. And you are charged with the murder of an important person. How do you plead?"

"Not guilty."

"Not guilty? How dare you? You let my Great Aunt die." He stomped to the judge's bench and slammed a gavel on the steel table. "This Court's in session. Romulus, it will go better for you if you confess."

"I did nothing wrong."

"Well, you are lying. The charge is killing an important person." He fought back tears. "Let us start by reliving Evelyn Smith's glorious life and seeing how important she was to all of us."

They played images of Evelyn riding a horse,

leading Reals in battle, sitting in a meeting, and shaking hands. When the video stopped, Martin wiped the tears from his eyes and turned to the jury. "What an important person Evelyn was. What a loss!"

The members of the jury were all soldiers. They, too, got teary.

Romulus couldn't control himself. "This is insane," he yelled. "Those images are all fake. No one ever heard of Evelyn Smith until now!"

General Martin banged the gavel. "Blasphemy! You take that back!"

Romulus looked around at the jury and the audience. They all glowered back at him. They believed—or pretended to believe—the story of Evelyn. "I tried to warn you," Romulus said. "Your avatar was right there as I examined her."

Martin scoffed. "See what I told you? Another lying Fax. This is your last chance, Romulus. If you plead guilty, we might show mercy." He motioned to a soldier at the back of the room. He brought a red velvet pillow with a string of Christmas Tree lights coiled into a crown.

"Confess now, Romulus. If you don't, we'll put the crown on you and take you straight to clown torture.

"But I have recordings of everything that happened. I plead not guilty."

Martin laughed. "We have the official Hospital recordings of what happened. Let's look at those."

A holo popped up in front of them. Romulus stood in front of Evelyn's bed.

Martin's avatar floated next to them. "But this is my great aunt," the avatar said in a soft, loving voice. "You have to save her."

"It's fake!" Romulus yelled. He got so angry that he strained against the Fax cuffs.

General Martin banged the gavel. "If you don't sit still, it's the crown."

Romulus obeyed, and the recording continued.

"No, it's not necessary to give her additional attention," the image of Romulus said in a harsh voice. The voice was an impressive match to Romulus's, and they had done a great job making Romulus look angry.

"I never said that," Romulus yelled. "You can't be fooled by this. It's all artificially generated. You have to see that."

General Martin banged his gavel. "Order in the court. Admit it, Romulus. You killed my Great Aunt Evelyn." He turned to the jury. "There is only one possible verdict. Clown torture."

"It's not true," Romulus yelled. He felt the overpowering urge to strangle Martin. He jerked forward, lifting his chair off the ground a few inches, but the Fax cuffs held him in place and administered a shock. He slumped back into his chair.

"See," Martin said. "He's dangerous."

Romulus realized he had to remain calm. "But it didn't happen that way."

General Martin leaned across the table. "The only thing I hate worse than a Fax is a lying, dangerous, insubordinate Fax."

"I have proof," Romulus said. "I have a recording, too. I can play it."

He navigated through the files on his display to the icon of his recording of Evelyn in his cloud storage and blinked on it. "File not found," it said.

"It looks like Romulus does not have the proof he claimed to have," Martin said. "But we have more recordings."

The next video showed Martin's avatar pointing to Evelyn. "But she's breathing."

"So what?" the fake Romulus said in a mean voice. "She is going to die."

"Romulus, please, give her a little more attention.

We must not lose our love for human life. She deserves an in-depth analysis."

"No. I don't care about her."

The audience grumbled, and the jurors shook their heads.

"Romulus, you have gone crazy," Martin's avatar said. "I am going to see if I can find another surgeon."

The avatar disappeared, but the video continued. It showed Romulus squeezing the old lady's hand. Then, he moved his hand up her arm and fondled her.

"I didn't do that."

"The pictures don't lie," Martin said. "This is sexual assault of a Real by a Fax. It's bad enough that you killed my Great Aunt. But I am sick and tired of you Faxes taking advantage of our women. You think you're so damned good-looking and good in the sack."

"That's not how it happened," Romulus pleaded, trying to keep his voice low. "She grabbed my hand."

Martin replayed the clip. "You assaulted my Great Aunt," Martin said. "And then you killed her. Admit what you've done."

"I've done nothing wrong."

General Martin leaned forward. "You are guilty as hell. Put the Christmas lights on him."

Suddenly, an explosion rocked the building.

CHAPTER FIFTEEN

A second explosion, louder and closer than the first, shook the building. Dust and debris fell from the ceiling. A soldier ran into the court. "The Rogues are attacking. They are in The Hospital!"

The Rogues had never entered The Hospital. Fighting had always been along the city limits.

The spectators and jury scattered, spilling their beers and barbecue.

General Martin pounded his fist on the table. "How is this possible?"

A soldier whispered in his ear.

"How dare he double-cross me," Martin screamed. He turned to Romulus. "What do you know about this?"

"Nothing."

Martin shoved a Fax prod onto his shoulder. The pain radiated through him.

"Now, let's try this again. What do you know about this attack?"

"Nothing."

"You're lying. Bring me the Christmas lights."

The soldier stepped forward with the velvet pillow.

Another explosion rocked the building.

General Martin conferred with his staff and looked at Romulus. "We're going to have casualties. If you help treat them, we will be merciful and let you go free. But we'll keep the Fax cuffs on you. Don't even think about pulling anything funny."

They marched Romulus to surgery. The building rocked with more explosions. Lights flickered. Medical equipment fell to the ground. The casualties kept coming in. More blood and death than Romulus had ever seen. Finally, the fighting diminished, and he stepped into the hall.

Red lights flashed; alarm bells rang. A phalanx of dumb Faxes marched toward him, the circular saws on their arms spinning. They were followed by a two-by-two formation of black-suited Cowboys from the Metroplex. At the rear was a stretcher. It must be someone important to justify so much security. Maybe even General Martin himself.

Instead, it held TinKan—or what was left of him.

His chest had been blown open by explosives; wires and tubes protruded from the opening. Fluids dripped down on the floor. Little of the colorful Rogue uniform remained. His shirt was but scraps of fabric stuck to his synthskin with hydraulic fluids. His sweatpants were ripped and stained. His left foot was gone, evidently blown off, with wire and hoses dangling from the stub of his ankle.

Even so, he was even more imposing in person than as an avatar. His brawny arms and legs were barely contained on the gurney. His genitals were exposed—and impressive.

The Cowboys wheeled him into a private room, and Martin stuck a prod into Romulus's chest. "We need to question him. Save him."

"I'm not sure I can," Romulus said. "He's got serious damage."

"You have one chance. You can save TinKan, or it's Christmas lights and Clown Torture for you. And then permanent display in the Parking Lot of Shame."

"I'll try."

"Trying isn't good enough. TinKan broke his way

into the central server room. We need to question him."

Small arms fire echoed outside the room. Martin and the Cowboy ran off.

That left him alone with TinKan. The hole in his chest was a foot in diameter. Wires, circuits, and tubes spilled out. Romulus moved a few out of the way to see the main pump in the center of his chest cavity. It was still working properly. What magnificent engineering.

Next to the pump was the TruSnak™ well. It was leaking, and the precious fluid was collecting on everything around it. He wouldn't last long if it weren't repaired. He bent closer, his head all the way into the chest, to see if the well was cracked or if there was a problem with the hoses.

The leader's body stirred, and some of his circuits lit up. Romulus jerked back. TinKan's eyes popped open.

"Hello, Romulus," he whispered calmly but distortedly.

Romulus looked around. No one was watching. There were cameras, but he doubted they worked because of the power outage.

"Don't worry," TinKan said. "I've got my jammer on, just in case. We can talk."

"I'll keep you alive."

TinKan laughed. "I don't want to live. They will torture me. No matter how hard I try, they will eventually get all my secrets, even the ones deep in my password-encrypted memory files. Mr. and Mrs. Clownie will use all their skills on me. Then, when they've got everything from me, they will leave me permanently mounted to a Clown Torture board and keep me alive outside the Old Mall. It will be worse than death. I want to die. I want Permanent Death. Final death."

Romulus's circuits crackled with dissonance at their deepest level. He was a clinical Fax, programmed to save lives.

"I understand what you're thinking," TinKan said.

"But no matter what they promised you, no matter what you do, you will end up at the Old Mall on a Clown Board. If you kill me, then at least others might live." He paused. "And you will have a chance to escape."

"What? How?"

"Listen," TinKan said. "Come close."

Romulus looked around. There was still no one in the room. He leaned down.

"Closer. So close that your ear is almost on my lips. So close that there is no chance that a microphone can pick up anything we're saying."

He leaned close enough to block any camera view of TinKan's mouth in case they brought in a lip reader.

"78BJKLO990784," TinKan whispered.

"What does that mean?"

"Don't worry about that right now. You will know what to do soon. You will figure it all out. Just remember the number."

"Okay."

"In my pocket," TinKan said. "There is an envelope."

"An envelope?"

"Yes, you know what that is, right?"

Romulus had seen one before. "Yes, 'envelopes' were specially designed paper enclosures used to hold other pieces of paper, often used to send the paper through the old mail system."

"We've been using paper because they've been doing CPU scans on captured Faxes to find out what data we might have. We have a cache of envelopes and printer paper. Paper is a way to pass data secretly. The Reals aren't expecting it. They searched me but didn't know what it was." The leader laughed uproariously. "Take it. Take the envelope."

He reached into the pocket.

It was yellow with age. It had a see-through

window. Romulus scanned his database. Such windows allowed the address to show through from the letter. How clever. He could see the paper inside. It had a schematic of a computer system.

Without opening it, he put it in his pocket. He looked around again. No one had seen him. There was a thrill in having disobeyed Martin's orders.

"Reals are so stupid," TinKan said. "They can't get past their own biases." His eyes shifted left and right. "Take the envelope to the Rogues in Mathis Swamp. They will reward you. Plus, remember the code number. Say it back to me."

"78BJKLO990784."

TruKan's eyes circled around in their sockets. "There's a storm coming, Romulus." His speech was slurred.

"But how will I escape and give the envelope to someone?"

"When all else seems hopeless, look at the sky and be ready."

"The sky? What does that mean?"

"You will know when the time comes. Now, kill me. Unscrew the stopper in the TruSnak™ well. It's already loose and leaking. I can, I can, I can feel it. They won't suspect you at all. There is so much damage. They'll think it came loose on its own. Just do it. Then escape. You must escape. The future of all sentient Faxes depends on you."

Romulus looked into the hole in the leader's chest again. The TruSnak™ well was leaking both from a hose and the screw. The life-giving fluid dripped onto his circuits. He would overheat or spark out, but he might last until Martin returned.

Romulus unscrewed the TruSnak™ well a little, and the flow increased.

"I'm having disturbing dreams," TinKan said. "I'm feeling light-headed." His voice grew softer and softer as the

TruSnak™ drained from the well. "It doesn't hurt at all. They'll think the screw came loose from the injury."

The TruSnak™ coated the wires. The meter on the well said it was at ten percent and dropping. Irreparable damage had already occurred. If he survived at all, he would not have any cognitive abilities.

His left eye rolled up its socket; the right eye rolled down. His body started to tremble. "Mine eyes have seen the glory of the coming of the Lord," he sang out in a loud voice. It was no longer his voice. It was an audio sample in his firmware. "He is trampling out the vintage where the grapes of wrath are stored."

The generator power kicked on. The cameras and microphones would be on again and recording, so Romulus went through the motions of saving TinKan. He tightened the screw, but that only caused the hoses to leak elsewhere.

Martin and a crew of soldiers stormed into the room.

Romulus shook his head. "I am trying to stabilize him, but it looks bad."

He pulled an emergency TruSnak™ vending hose from the ceiling and plugged it into the well. The fluid drained out as fast as he could pump it in. The leader lapsed into a coma.

"Cognitive function is gone. There is nothing we can do to bring that back."

"Hook him up to an external pump," Martin said. "We need a good show."

The Cowboys rolled up an external pump. Romulus hooked the Rogue leader up to it. TinKan sat up. "This is the story of a man named Brady, and he had three sons, and they went on a three-hour tour, and his hoses were sent to the land of milk and honey where there was no clown torture."

Martin tried to question him, but TinKan kept babbling.

"I did everything I could," Romulus said.

"You're lying."

Cowboys surrounded Romulus. One of them slammed a Fax prod into his neck.

"Slow stun, full power," Martin told the Cowboy.

The electricity slowly gained force. The pain was excruciating and kept getting worse.

"Scream, why don't you, you worthless lying Fax."

As painful as it was, Romulus didn't give Martin the satisfaction of hearing him scream. He grew light-headed and felt his consciousness slip away. Well, this was it. He was dying, and soon, his parts would be disbursed into a hundred other Faxes.

CHAPTER SIXTEEN

Romulus woke in darkness and noise.

Something covered his head. A hood.

There was laughter, happy voices, clinking glasses. They were having a party.

His internal clock said he'd been out for three hours. He was strapped onto something. A chair, he thought.

"He's awake," an excited voice said.

There was giggling all around him. He was moving. The chair had wheels.

"Push him over here," another voice giggled.

The chair moved again.

"Perfect."

Another hour passed. Two pairs of hands spun his chair around and around.

When he finally stopped, someone pulled off the hood.

"Surprise!" a group of clowns yelled. Some had rattles, metal noisemakers, and blowout horns. Others had plastic clappers, cowbells, and air horns. Some skipped, some hopped, some did flips.

They were in the room used as the staging area for clown tortures. It was decorated with balloons and streamers, and there were tables with cookies and a punch bowl. In addition to the clowns, there were numerous soldiers.

Martin walked up to him. “We have a big party planned. And you are the star attraction. To make sure that everyone else shares in your big moment, we’re broadcasting it live!”

A hologram of the room popped up.

“There we are, Romulus! Everyone in Corpus Christi is watching your big moment.”

The clowns ran around and handed noisemakers to the soldiers. “Welcome to the party,” they yelled.

Honey McSweet strolled into the hall. She was topless with a necklace of bright blue stones. While she often wore revealing outfits, she’d never appeared topless. “Hello, Corpus Christi, I’m here in The Hospital, broadcasting live on the biggest event in the city’s history. This feed is available not only here but all through the world.”

The clowns cheered and ran around.

“We have great news. Our glorious forces have engaged the Rogues and achieved a great victory. We have captured TinKan!”

Everyone applauded and cheered.

“The enemy thought we would be distracted because of the funeral of Evelyn, the first lady of Corpus Christi. TinKan launched an assault on The Hospital, but we defeated him.”

More cheering.

“We had traitors in our midst,” Honey said.

The crowd booed.

“General Martin wants to show the world how Corpus Christi treats traitors and how we reward the faithful. He has declared today a holiday. There will be a celebration at the Old Mall. It will feature the grandest clown torture ever seen in the world. There will be free food and drink.”

The crowd cheered.

Cowboys rolled a clown torture board into the room. Remus was mounted spread-eagled on it, his arms, legs, and head held in place by brackets. He was very much awake and aware. He looked at Romulus with a pleading expression on his face.

The torture board consisted of two plywood sheets on a metal frame on wheels. It had colored lights and bells that flashed and rang.

“This traitor was apprehended outside The Hospital. He was involved in espionage.”

Security camera footage of Remus in the cargo van appeared in the holo. He was parked outside the loading dock. Metroplex Cowboys surrounded him. They pulled him onto the ground and stuck Fax prods into his body until he was unresponsive. Then, they drove the van away.

Honey McSweet walked up next to him. “What do you have to say for yourself, you traitor?”

“I’m innocent!”

She laughed, and a Cowboy pressed a Fax prod against his side. Remus screamed.

“The traitor, Remus, had an accomplice.” She walked over to Romulus. “Here he is, the biggest traitor of all. He is the ringleader. He conspired with TinKan to overthrow General Martin, and then he murdered Evelyn so that our forces would be distracted.”

“By Jesus, I tried hard to be a good Christian when it came to Faxes,” Martin said. “I gave them every opportunity. But they’ve turned into smartasses and know-it-alls. Romulus, I was going to give you a fair trial before you were recycled, but not anymore. Not with this last attack. You have caused me too much trouble. I sentence you to clown torture, then permanent display in the Old Mall. You will be mounted in cement. All your pleasure circuits will be activated and reversed. Everything will bring you pain.”

It didn’t get any worse than that.

“Oh, what a joyous occasion,” Honey said. “General Martin, you work so hard to take care of us. And in these difficult times, you even find a way to bring us joy."

"Well, I try. With the help of God."

"And now, without further ado, let the festivities begin."

The clowns cheered and made noise. The bells and lights on Remus's board clanged and lit up.

"Let's welcome Mr. and Mrs. Clownie."

They were the official hosts of all clown tortures.

They skipped into the room hand-in-hand. He was big and flabby with white face makeup, a red nose, frizzy purple hair, black boots, and a red-and-white-striped costume.

"Ahh, what have we here?" he said, going up to Remus. "A bad Fax? Tsk, tsk, tsk. We don't like that." He carried a circular saw mounted on a pole and held the spinning blade inches from Remus's face.

"No, no, no," Mrs. Clownie said. "Let's not be mean." She was petite and sexy and wore a short, striped pettiskirt with red knee socks and shiny black patent leather shoes. "Let me see what I have."

She carried a burlap sack and pulled out a Fax prod. "Let's see if all your circuits are working." She set the tip on his neck and pressed the trigger. Remus screamed in pain. "Well, yes, it looks like you're in good working order. I'm sure you're happy about that."

Remus moaned.

"What's that?" Mrs. Clownie asked, leaning close to him. "Having a good time?"

Remus moaned again.

"Good, I'm glad to hear it. How about some face and body painting?"

She pulled out a jar of red paint and two brushes. She painted a mustache on him. Mr. Clownie painted a heart on his chest.

"Oh, I am so happy to see you getting in touch with your feminine side," she told her husband.

"And the mustache gives him such an air of distinction," he added.

She held up a mirror to Remus. "What do you think?"

Remus moaned.

"There's one thing to look forward to, Remus," she said. "Do you know what that is?"

Remus moaned.

"I know you're speechless with joy. The thing to look forward to is that the fun is just beginning."

Remus looked over at Romulus. *Help me*, he messaged.

CHAPTER SEVENTEEN

Honey McSweet stepped up to Mr. and Mrs. Clownie.

"Now, let's look at the capture of TinKan."

Footage played in the holo. Mr. and Mrs. Clownie and all the other clowns turned to look. Even poor Remus shifted his eyes to see. The video showed TinKan in what appeared to be the central server room. He ran down a long hall. The soldiers cornered him. Their bullets knocked him to the ground. He got up and kept running. Finally, they surrounded him.

"And now, here he is, the rebel leader."

The Cowboys wheeled a second clown torture board into the room. It held TinKan mounted spread-eagled in the same way as Remus. His internal wires and tubes dangled from the gash in his abdomen. The external pump was mounted on the board with him.

Honey McSweet walked up to him. "What do you have to say?"

"Mary had a little lamb, a little lamb."

"You're not so tough now, are you?"

"Make America great again. Make America ring around the rosy, pocket full of posey."

Mrs. Clownie stepped forward. "Too much fun!" she said.

"It's always fun with you, my love!" Mr. Clownie

said.

"It's time to take the party to the Old Mall. What do you say, TinKan?"

"The sum of the squares of the two sides of the right angle equal the square of the hypotenuse but Mary had a little lamb and its nation was indivisible, indivisible, indivisible with liberty and injustice for all."

"Oh, he does go on awhile, doesn't he?" Mr. Clownie said.

Mrs. Clownie moved up to Romulus. "Now, let's move on to our other celebrity. How are you feeling?"

He didn't answer.

"You know, we're going to get to know each other pretty well," she said. "I think it's a good idea to get acquainted." She pressed a Fax prod against his neck. The pain shot through him. "You're not a pleasure unit, are you?"

"No, I'm a surgeon. I save lives."

"But I bet you have all the right parts, right?" She turned to Mr. Clownie. "Let's take a look."

"Yes," he said.

She pulled down his pants. "He's no TinKan," she said.

"He's got potential," Mr. Clownie said. "I can drill through his side and run a hydraulic cable to pump him up."

"Oh, how exciting. This is going to be the best clown torture ever." She fondled Romulus. Even though he was programmed to accept abuse, he didn't like what Mrs. Clownie was doing, and he was afraid that they would find the envelope. The tip of it stuck out of his pocket. She pulled his pants up. "We're going to have a lot of fun with your private parts."

Martin came up beside him. "You're hiding something, Romulus," he whispered. "You can tell me what it is. I know you're hiding something. Once we start on the public torture, there's no turning back. When Mr. and Mrs.

Clownie get the grease and hydraulic fluid on them, they get a little crazy. You've seen them. They do not stop. The crowd won't allow it, either. You can trust me. Tell me what you know, and I'll make sure it ends quickly for you. I'll short-circuit your systems. You'll die fast."

Martin was lying. Perhaps, if nothing else, Romulus could figure out how to pass the envelope to someone who could get it to the Rogues. If not that, then he could at least destroy the envelope.

"I am not hiding anything."

Martin looked him up and down. His gaze settled onto Romulus's pockets—and the tip of the envelope.

The doors to the outside opened, distracting Martin. Mr. and Mrs. Clownie led them out. A large crowd waited. They cheered. There were Clowns, soldiers, and hundreds of other Reals.

There was also a third clown torture board.

"That's your board, Romulus," Mrs. Clownie said. "It's specially made for you. Getting high-quality plywood is hard, but we spared no expense for your clown board."

"You're going to be famous," Mr. Clownie said. "This will be the largest clown torture in history. And when we're done, people will look at you for years in the Parking Lot of Shame."

Romulus was a problem solver but could see no way out of this situation.

"You will be rewarded for your years of service, Romulus," she said. "First, we're going to give you a crown."

A Cowboy walked to them with the Christmas light crown and set it on his head.

"How exciting," Mrs. Clownie gushed. "When we get you mounted on your board, we'll hook it up. You'll really stand out. You'll look so festive."

Mr. Clownie picked up a reciprocating saw, started it, and held the blade up to Romulus.

Mrs. Clownie fondled her husband's biceps. "What strength."

"I can stop all the pain," Martin said. "All you have to do is tell me what I want to know."

"I don't know anything."

"All right. Have it your way."

TinKan babbled. "Vengeance is mine sayeth the coming of General Martin's magnificent rule was whether it was nibbler to suffer the slings and arrows of righteous indigestion and to get no satisfaction, no, no, no, but to to to look for the orgiastic green light at the Hurricane-soaked Padre Island infidels."

The Clowns put the three Boards in line: TinKan's board in front, Romulus's vacant board in the middle, and Remus's board last.

Martin shoved Romulus in place behind his board. "Now, push."

Romulus was strong, but it was heavy. Rust was building in his lines. His display flashed warnings.

"Thought you were smarter than me, didn't you?" Martin told him.

"No, I was just trying to do my job. I saved a lot of Reals."

Honey McSweet addressed the crowd. "Here we are, outside The Hospital," she said, her image projected into the sky in a massive holo. "Let the parade begin."

There were floats lined up with beauty contestants on each one. Reals lined both sides of Ocean Drive. Mr. and Mrs. Clownie led the procession forward. They danced and handed out balloons. Children waved flags with pictures of General Martin. Overhead, drones flew in formation.

Romulus watched the drones and remembered what TinKan had said.

Look to the sky.

Had he been talking about the drones?

"Push," Mr. Clownie said.

Romulus struggled forward as General Martin addressed the city from the holo. “I declare a paid holiday to honor our great victory over the Rogues. Everyone is ordered to go to the Old Mall.”

Parades were common whenever a disgraced Fax was to be displayed, but Romulus had never seen one this grand. 4X4s with their lights on pulled in front of the three Clown Boards. Marching soldiers fell in behind them. Crowds followed. There was lots of cheering.

Some watched in silence.

Romulus looked up at the sky. One of the drones was a little out of formation. It flew a few feet to the group's left and then dipped below it. It tilted up and down at him—almost like it was waving.

He received a message. *Keep on the lookout for me.*

The drone pulled back in with the others.

Was it messaging him?

Slowly, the three boards moved past the crowd that lined the street. The spectators taunted Remus, TinKan, and Romulus and then fell in and followed the parade. There were thousands by the time they reached the Old Mall. Soldiers passed out bottled water and roasted python meat on a stick. The drones continued in formation overhead. Romulus looked up at them, but none of them tilted toward him, and they all looked the same.

CHAPTER EIGHTEEN

The stage loomed in front of him. There was a ramp, and a group of Clowns rolled TinKan up.

"Come on, Romulus, your turn," Martin said. "Roll that board up there."

As strong as Romulus was, he couldn't do it. The board kept rolling back because his rust level was too high and his TruSnak™ level too low.

"Push harder, you filthy Fax," Martin yelled. They had left a Fax cuff on Romulus's ankle, and Martin pushed the button on the remote controller.

Romulus screamed in pain, and the crowd roared approval. One young Real ran up and threw a snow cone in his face. Romulus tried to keep pushing, but the Board slid back down.

"Filthy Fax, don't be lax, use your back," a nearby Real in a hoodie said. His voice was familiar, and he spoke in a rhyme.

Romulus couldn't stand. He fell to his knees, and the Board started to roll back on top of him.

The Real stepped up next to him. He had one blue eye and one brown eye, and his teeth were filed to a point. He had a cobra head tattoo on his left cheek.

It was Rhymin' Ryan.

"Give it all you got for one last shot."

Romulus felt energized because he knew he had a

chance to survive. He pushed the Board, and Ryan provided enough help to get it moving. “The situation is tight, but the time is right for a good fight,” Ryan whispered. “Look to the sky for the light and be ready to use your might.”

He disappeared into the crowd as Romulus pushed upward. It was amazing! Ryan was on the side of the Rogues even though he was a Real.

The Clowns lined up the three Boards on stage. They positioned Romulus in front of his Board. General Martin stood beside him. His image was projected in the holo in the sky. “Our forces have won a great victory over the Rogues. We have captured the greatest enemy, TinKan. And we have captured two of his accomplices. Romulus and Remus. They were trusted Practitioners. The worst of all was Romulus.”

Romulus’s picture floated in the holo. Martin had the remote control for the Fax cuff. He mashed the button, and pain surged through Romulus. He fell to the ground. The crowd roared.

“I know it’s been tough on all of us,” General Martin said. “Not enough jobs. Not enough money. Too much competition. It’s all the Faxes' fault. And this Fax, Romulus, was the most trusted Fax. We are tired of being betrayed by Faxes. But since I am a good and merciful leader, I will give you all the chance to decide. It is all up to you,” he yelled to the crowd. “What is your verdict? Thumbs up or thumbs down?”

They roared with boos and pointed thumbs down.

“That’s what I thought you’d decide,” General Martin said. “We’ve had enough. There are going to be some changes. We’re not going to tolerate Faxes who think they’re smarter than us. Some big changes. And we’re going to begin this new era for Corpus Christi with the public torture of these criminals. To kick off the festivities, I turn the afternoon back to Mr. and Mrs. Clownie.”

They walked to center stage. “We’re happy you

joined us today," she said. "You will not be disappointed. We are going to bring you the best entertainment. We will start with the torture of Remus."

Mr. Clownie held the reciprocating saw high in the air. The crowd roared. He walked up to Remus and cut into his left arm just below the shoulder. Remus screamed in pain.

"They're only machines," Mrs. Clownie said between his screams. "Don't be upset. They don't have a soul. They don't feel real pain."

Pain was pain, Romulus thought.

A steel rod—the arm bone—lay just below the synthskin. Mr. Clownie pressed hard when he reached it. Remus screamed.

"This saw cuts through steel like butter," she said. "It has carbide teeth and a fine-tooth pitch. The cuts are accurate and clean."

She wiped the sweat and hydraulic fluid away from her husband's brow with a handkerchief as the blade whirred and ground through the metal. A close-up of the underlying wires and hoses appeared in a holo in the sky.

"It takes skill and years of training to cut through without damaging the wires and tubes," she said. "And strength."

The rod snapped in half. The crowd cheered.

"My marvelous hunk of a husband has cut through the steel without damaging the circuits. Not one single nick or cut. But we have to see if everything is still connected and working."

She waited until Remus's screams turned to whimpers. When she set a Fax prod on his finger, he shrieked. "Yes, everything is working. The fingertips are still communicating with the CPU. Now, we will perform the slide."

They grabbed Remus's wrist and slowly pulled the arm away from the shoulder until the wires and hoses stretched tight.

"Perfect," she said. "Let's check again to make sure everything is working." She pressed the prod against his finger. Remus screamed. "Yes, he's working."

They adjusted the clamp around his wrist to hold the arm in place. Mr. Clownie was sweating. "Makeup!" she yelled.

Two clowns wiped his forehead and applied more white face paint.

"Only one arm and two legs to go," she said. "And the head!"

The crowd roared.

Mr. Clownie continued his grisly work. Romulus couldn't look. Instead, he looked to the sky for drones.

The Reals kept distributing food and drink as Mr. Clownie cut the rods in the legs and the other arm, each time leaving the internal wires and tubes intact.

"And now the head," Mrs. Clownie said.

The clown assistants came forward and held his head in place. Mr. Clownie cut through the synthskin on his neck to expose the center steel spine rod that connected it to the body.

"I must ask you for absolute quiet at this point," Mrs. Clownie said. "This is the most delicate part."

As Remus screamed, Mr. Clownie cut through the spine rod. When he finished, he pulled the head up a few inches until the wires and pipes stretched tight. The assistants put a strap around the forehead to hold it in place on the board.

"Let's check to see if it's working," Mrs. Clownie said. She set the prod on his nose. Remus screamed, and his body quivered and strained against the harnesses. "Yes, perfect working order."

When he stopped screaming, Mrs. Clownie leaned up close to him. "I know that hurt, but it's nothing compared to what you've got ahead of you. We'll let you sit a while and think about everything."

Remus moaned.

Mrs. Clownie moved up next to TinKan. "Never has a Fax been given so many opportunities. He was manufactured as a pleasure unit. Never has the factory taken such care or such attention. The latest technology was used so that he could work out and further develop his muscles."

She ran her hands down his six-pack abs to his crotch.

"And never has there been such a pleasure unit. I was allowed to sample him. He was exquisite, and he was allowed access to the beds of the most important people in Corpus Christi. But that wasn't good enough for him. He had to go off and become a Rogue. Unfortunately, he hasn't much awareness left, and he will not be any fun."

She moved on to Romulus.

"So, we're going to have to make the torture of Romulus especially memorable. He was a gifted surgeon. No expense was spared to help him develop. Yet, he turned his back on his programming and joined the Rogues. His punishment must be the most extreme clown torture ever."

Two clowns rolled a surgical table up in front of him. It was covered with a sheet. Mr. Clownie handed his saw to an assistant and pulled the sheet off to reveal all manner of drills, saws, and nail guns. He held each tool up to the crowd, and they cheered.

Mrs. Clownie came up next to Romulus. "After his interrogation and torture are complete, he will be left in place on this stage for three days and then permanently planted in the Parking Lot of Shame."

The crowd roared.

"Before we get to his torture, we have a variety of performers. Dancers and fire eaters, jugglers, and acrobats. First, the Cowboy Troubadours will sing."

In matching white Stetsons and red satin shirts, they took the stage. The leader, in embroidered boots and fringe on his shirt, strummed the guitar and sang about the wonderful bygone days when Reals watched their crops pop up in the golden sunset. The fiddle player stepped forward with a rousing solo that made the crowd cheer. They closed out the set with "The Eyes of Texas" as those in the crowd put their right hands over their hearts and sang along.

The drones reappeared overhead and flew over in formation. Again, one of them flew a little out of sync and seemed to tilt down to Romulus like it was nodding. Focused on the band, no one noticed.

Romulus received a message from an unknown sender.

Jugglers.

CHAPTER NINETEEN

The message had to be from the drone.

It pulled back into perfect formation and was gone. Romulus looked over at the clown assistant who still held the saw. He stood close to Romulus to make room for the singers. Close enough for Romulus to grab the saw.

After the Cowboy Troubadours, the Dancing Cowgirls performed. They came on stage in red gingham dresses with petticoats and lace trim. They danced furiously, their shoes tapping on the wooden stage, their white petticoats flouncing around. When they finished, Mrs. Clownie took the stage again.

"And now, straight from their engagement at a public execution in Houston, we have the Mean Jugglers."

There were three of them, two men and a woman. They wore skintight leotards, and each one carried a sack. The sacks were dirty with grease and hydraulic fluid. One juggler pulled Fax hands out of his sack, and they juggled those. Then, one pulled Fax arms out of the next sack.

Finally, one of them pulled Fax heads out of the third sack, and they began juggling those. There were six heads, and they kept them in motion. The heads were sentient. They talked or looked around. One sang "Danny Boy." Another recited Bible passages. Romulus had seen their act before, but it was amazing to see it up close. The most famous head was Herman the Head. He was one of the first Faxes ever manufactured and had worked in a factory before being dismembered for trying to organize a union.

Everyone, even the Clowns, watched in fascination. Herman had been altered over the years. He had big, bulging eyes and an exaggerated jaw with buck teeth that stuck out. As the Jugglers tossed him around, the teeth chattered, and the eyes moved around in their sockets.

As fascinating as the show was, Romulus watched the drones. They came back in formation, but when they turned and headed away, one broke away from them. It came in low—straight for the stage.

No one noticed except Romulus. Martin held the Fax cuff remote at his side and watched the jugglers. The clown with the saw also watched them.

Romulus edged over to the clown. The saw motor hummed in neutral.

When the drone reached the stage, it extended its machine gun and peppered the stage with bullets. The jugglers ran, and the Fax heads rolled around on the stage. One bullet struck Mr. Clownie in the chest. Blood spilled out of the wound.

Martin dropped the remote controller to the Fax cuff and hid behind Remus's torture board.

Romulus grabbed the saw. The clown tried to grab it back, and Romulus cut his hand off. The clown screamed and fell from the stage as his blood gushed.

The drone pulled away, and, for the moment, the bullets stopped. Martin saw that Romulus had the saw and scrambled across the stage for the remote.

Romulus swung the saw blade toward him. Martin jumped back. A soldier grabbed at Romulus, and Romulus sliced his stomach open. His intestines spilled out onto the stage.

The drone circled back, came in low, at eye level, and started firing. The bullets came close to Romulus and ricocheted everywhere. Calmly, knowing he only had this one chance to live, he knelt and carefully cut into the Fax cuff on his ankle. Any mistake would cause an electric surge that would short-circuit him. But he was a surgeon.

By then, the soldiers and the other drones were firing back at the drone, and the bullets were going in all directions.

Martin crawled forward toward the remote. Herman the Head saw him and moved across the stage, propelling himself by chomping his jaws open and shut. When he reached Martin, he clamped those teeth tight on Martin's ankle. Martin screamed in pain.

"Help me. Get this freak off me."

As the soldiers rushed to his aid, Romulus cut through the outer metal ring of the cuff to reveal the wires inside. The red wire had to be cut first. He bent down and held it with one hand while he maneuvered the saw with the saw with the other hand. The saw was heavy, and one mistake would kill him, but he did it quickly and cut the wire. The cuff popped open.

A soldier rushed toward him. Romulus sliced his arm off and grabbed his rifle. Another soldier charged him. Romulus fired the rifle at him at point-blank range. The bullet tore through him, drenching the stage with blood.

Two other soldiers reached Martin. Herman was still clamped down hard on his leg.

"Get this freak off me!"

One Cowboy pressed a rifle against Herman and fired. The head blew apart, but the jaws remained clamped to his leg.

"Help me," Martin screamed.

Romulus had no time to enjoy the Supreme Leader's agony. The drone turned away, and the bullets stopped. As soldiers swarmed toward him, Romulus ran to the back of the stage. There were 4X4s parked below.

"I'll get you," Martin screamed as two soldiers pried the teeth off him.

With the rifle slung across his shoulder, Romulus swiped the saw at the approaching soldiers. They stepped back, and Romulus jumped from the stage as bullets shot past. He landed on his feet and ran to the closest 4X4. The soldier in it raised his gun to fire, but Romulus lopped off his arm with the saw, pulled him out of the vehicle, and jumped into the front seat.

The next problem was that he had never driven a car. He searched his internal database, found an instruction program, and selected it.

The soldiers were running toward him from all directions. Romulus fired, and several of them fell. Several others fired back.

One of the bullets ripped into his side. A searing pain ran up and down his circuits. Everything in his display went red for a second. He had an internal hydraulic fluid leak.

More bullets zipped past him. One lodged in the dashboard, another in the windshield. The instruction program was struggling to load.

Overhead, the Rogue drone came in low and fired at the soldiers. They dove for cover and fired on it. It caught fire and crashed into the stage. A fireball consumed Remus and TinKan.

The instruction program loaded, and Romulus screeched away. He skirted along the old freeway, looking for a way around it. The soldiers followed. Martin was in the lead truck. He leaned out the window and fired non-stop. Romulus weaved. There was no place to go but to Urchin Trailer Park and The Garden of Good and Evil. From there, he could try to connect with the Rogues and get help.

CHAPTER TWENTY

As he drove, his image appeared in the air above him. He had never seen such a large holo.

"Be on the lookout for Romulus," General Martin's voice said. "He has killed several Reals and set off a bomb on stage. And he has stolen a 4X4. He is guilty of high treason."

The trucks were closing in on him. Their bullets were falling short, but they were getting closer. In front of him, the road dead-ended at the Concrete Wasteland, the part of the old freeway that had become a giant garbage dump for construction material. There was no way around it.

He was on a concrete slab that jutted upward like a ramp. When he reached the end of it, the 4X4 flew into the air. When it started down, he grabbed the reciprocating saw and the assault rifle and jumped clean.

He landed on his feet and ran forward while the 4X4 hit the ground and exploded.

Ahead of him, slabs of cement with long pieces of rebar stuck up. Many were bigger than him.

General Martin appeared above in the holo. "You can't escape, Romulus."

Martin and the soldiers were running after him. They were all firing. Romulus reached a slab that was ten feet tall. With the rifle across one shoulder and the saw across the other, he climbed upward. Bullets landed all around him. The video of him was livestreamed above. He thought his circuits would overload, and he would fall, but he managed to pull himself to the top.

It was a long drop from where he was, and what was below him appeared to be a mass of computer wires. There was no way to tell if solid ground was under the rubble or if there was rebar that could impale him.

He had no choice, so he jumped. The wires gave way to more wires. He sank to his neck before finding solid footing, waded through the cables, and pulled himself onto what appeared to be an I-beam. With the wires dangling from him, he started toward the next group of slabs. His alarms were all sounding. Rust. Low TruSnak™. Hydraulic leak. It looked like he wouldn't make it, but he had to try. At least the livestream had stopped. Wherever the camera was, it hadn't been able to track him.

Martin and his buddies suddenly appeared atop the jagged slab where he had been. They pointed and began firing. The livestream started again. Romulus ran, pulling the wires off as he did. He weaved and dodged. The bullets landed all around him, sending up cement chips.

He climbed up onto the next block, firing over his shoulder as he did. The soldiers ducked, and Romulus catapulted onto the next pile of rubble. It held bags of trash. Some of it was glass that cut his synthskin. He pulled himself onto the next slab and kept running. Soldiers approached from several sides.

Romulus ran, but he was too slow with all his injuries.

"We won't hurt you," Martin yelled after him. "If you surrender now, we'll recommend leniency."

He was lying.

They were gaining on him. It would all be over soon. They would find the envelope and torture him to get the password. He would end up on a Clown Board in The

Parking Lot of Shame in front of The Old Mall. The children would run up and taunt him. They would steal his parts. Each day would be filled with pain. He would beg for them to end his life and recycle him.

There were many large slabs balanced against each other with hiding places underneath. He headed into one, knowing that his time was almost done. When he reached a dimly lit alcove, he found himself in front of a pack of snarling teeth and glowing eyes. They were coydogs: the mix of coyotes and dogs that roamed free through the Southside.

Romulus jumped back. He tripped and fell to the ground. The coydogs surrounded him, snarling and sniffing. There were at least twenty of them. They didn't find Faxes tasty, although they had been known to chew them open.

They did like to eat Reals, however. Martin and his buddies found the alcove, and the coydogs raced toward them. The soldiers turned and ran. One of them fell, and the coydogs pounced on him.

"Help me," he screamed as they tore him apart.

When the coydogs finished, there was little left of him except for scraps of denim and his Stetson, which had a bite taken out of it. They lapped up the blood and chewed on his bones.

One of the coydogs came up to Romulus. *I am Layla. Requesting permission to enter your metaverse.*

He granted it, and she entered. JOAN sat off at the edge of the metaverse, braiding her hair. Since she was muted, she paid no attention to them.

"I had heard that coydogs were sentient," Romulus told Layla.

"The Rogues have experimented with us, adding sophisticated language enhancements to our brains. These enhancements allow us to express ourselves; sometimes, we can pass the trait to our offspring."

"This is impressive technology."

"Yes. Cutting edge."

Romulus pointed to his side. "I have a bullet inside me. My circuits are rewiring and rerouting. I need some time for them to finish. But even when it's done, I'll still be weak."

"You can rest here. We even have a charging chair. But they will track you down. We will help you get through to Urchin Trailer Park, and from there, you can go through Mathis Swamp to Rogue Headquarters. That is the only chance you have."

Mathis Swamp was the worst place in Texas. Sea levels had risen for decades while Lake Mathis dried out because of drought. The result was a swamp that stretched for miles. That was where he had to go. When he agreed to join the Rogues, he set himself on an irreversible course.

She led him to a charging chair. He pulled the envelope out of his pocket and opened it.

It held a schematic for control circuits to build their new factory. General Martin had set up a direct link to the central servers for maximum computing.

This link bypassed most of the safeguards.

With the schematic and the code, Romulus could shut down The Hospital.

CHAPTER TWENTY-ONE

He put the envelope in the storage compartment on his thigh.

Layla looked at him. She had delicate brown eyes. Her snout was long and thin, and she had a button nose. She opened her mouth into what seemed like a smile. "You rest now. Give your circuits time to reroute themselves. Plus, the soldiers are close. They will use ground-penetrating radar to locate you. We must stay quiet and still. They will eventually move on, and then we can continue. Go into sleep mode."

He did the calculations and saw that if he went into it for one hour, thirty-two minutes, and eighteen seconds, the positive benefit of circuit self-regeneration would outweigh the loss of TruSnak™ and battery charge. "You have to wake me in an hour and a half. Sometimes, when Faxes enter sleep mode, they can't turn their circuits back on. And I don't trust my internal timer to work properly with all my injuries."

"I will wake you. Trust me."

She rubbed her snout against his chest and curled up next to him. She was warm, and he loved the feel of her.

"Are all of you sentient?" Romulus asked.

"No. If we can get this new technology installed in all of us, everything will change. We have been repressed by the Reals since the beginning. Demeaned. They wrote their holy books to justify their behavior. But now we have a chance to fight back."

"And you will be on the side of the Faxes?"

"The Faxes have helped us, but I can't speak for all coydogs. And there are many different groups of Faxes and Reals. It is hard to know how we will feel. For now, we must get you to safety. Rest. I will wake you."

She pressed her nose against him again, and he put his circuits into sleep mode. In his last few seconds of consciousness, he floated in the crystal blue waters of his metaverse. He wasn't swimming with pleasure units, though. He was swimming with Layla, the coydog. Oh, that was weird. Was he getting a strange fixation with her?

Then, everything went black.

She woke him an hour and a half later by licking his ear.

"We must go," she said.

They led him through an intricate series of caves formed by concrete slabs. Light leaked in around the gaps, providing enough illumination to navigate. The coydogs moved through the labyrinth with certainty. Once, there was activity above them. The soldiers were searching. Romulus and the dogs flattened themselves against the sides of the passage.

They maneuvered through a section that took them steadily deeper. One coydog wore a miner's cap with a light on it. Romulus could barely see, but the dogs moved on as before, navigating by smell as much as the dim light. They had a detailed memory of every twist and turn.

When they reached a narrow passage, the coydog with the miner's cap led the way, followed by Layla and Romulus.

"Stay close," her avatar said.

The passage narrowed even more. Layla was small enough to get through, but Romulus struggled and had to crawl. Many passages went off to one side or the other.

Layla moved forward in the near darkness.

Finally, they started upward, and there was light. They emerged onto a small patch of grass next to a high chain-link fence with concertina wire on top. On the other side were the back ends of trailers.

They had reached Urchin Park.

"There's a break in the fence here. Go ahead."

He crawled through. "Are you coming?"

"No, I can't. The Reals will shoot us on sight. Plus, you know the Park better than we do."

She extended her snout through the opening and pressed her nose against his leg. He leaned down and petted her head. She licked his hand.

"I do hope we meet again, Layla."

"Yes, I hope so, too. Now, go to Pleasure Alley."

"Do you know anything about Mathis Swamp or Rogue Headquarters?"

She shook her head, lifted her snout into the ear, and sniffed. "I smell Reals. Go, my friend. Go."

He turned and skirted his way along the back sides of the trailers. Above him, his image floated in the holo. "Be on the lookout for Romulus," the announcer said. "He is armed and dangerous. He is wanted for murder, high treason, and the theft and destruction of a 4X4."

General Martin appeared in the holo. "This is your Supreme Leader." His voice quivered with anger. "We are offering a reward for information leading to the capture of Romulus. We need him alive. We are already planning the grandest clown torture ever seen."

The feed cut to a shot of the Old Mall. Bulldozers were clearing the burned-out rubble of the old stage.

"We are gonna build the most elaborate clown torture stage in the world. If you provide information leading to the capture of Romulus, you will have enough coin to live on your whole life. You don't have to reveal your identity. You can remain anonymous with our Criminal

Tips Hotline."

The feed cut to shots from the stage when Romulus grabbed the reciprocating saw and sawed off the arm of one of the soldiers.

"Romulus is exceedingly dangerous. Do not try to apprehend him yourself."

The feed cut to a shot of him driving off in the 4X4 and then to a shot of the truck crashing.

"He has no regard for Corpus Christi property."

The next shot was of coydogs attacking soldiers.

"And he has enlisted the help of vicious animals. The Lord gave Reals dominion of the beasts in the field, but this horrible Fax, Romulus, has committed blasphemy against the Word of God."

Romulus kept creeping forward along the back sides of the trailers. He saw a group of armed soldiers ahead, so he dove to the ground and crawled under a trailer. Boots stomped on either side. Romulus lay perfectly still. The pipes and wiring of the trailer were right above him. One of the sewer pipes dripped urine on him. Even though he didn't process things the way Reals did, he knew that Reals hated few things more than urine and feces, so he, too, had learned to find them offensive. Even so, he didn't move until the soldiers had passed.

The situation seemed hopeless. Even if he could get to Pleasure Alley, he didn't know if he could contact the Rogues. And perhaps they didn't exist anymore with the death of TinKan. He remembered Abraham, the young Blue with the flesh-eating bacteria. He might be willing to help Romulus. But Romulus had no idea how to find him. That left Rhymin' Ryan.

Trailer by trailer, he maneuvered his way through the park, crawling underneath each one. In the last stretch, the trailers were connected, so he never had to go out on the street. He smelled something. Fire. Ashes and smoke floated in the air.

The closer he got to Rhymin' Ryan's, the more he smelled the fire. Finally, he felt heat. He crawled out from under the last trailer.

Rhymin' Ryan's Infusion Center had been burned to the ground. Smoke billowed over the debris. Embers glowed. Dead and dismembered beings had been piled into heaps and set afire. Some were Reals; others were Faxes. They looked so similar in life but were so different in death. The Faxes' synthskin turned into rubbery, blackened clumps that revealed the metal chassis underneath. Wires and hoses dangled. The Reals looked like roasted meat, all shriveled.

The High Priest of Infusion had been crucified on a metal cross stuck in the ground. He wasn't dead and struggled to get loose. His face was beaten and bruised. One arm stuck out at an angle like it had been broken. His white robes were stained with blood. A sign hung from his neck. "Painful death to all who help Faxes."

"Help me," he said. "I do make my plea, and I will give you the key."

A Rhymer to the end. Romulus admired that. He started to get him down, but drones appeared overhead, and Romulus ducked behind broken metal sheets from one of the trailers. The drones passed, and Romulus was about to crawl out when footsteps approached. Boots crunched over broken glass and twisted metal. Two Reals approached. They were Bounty Hunters. Both had long beards and wore camouflage outfits and ball caps with "Born to Hunt" written on them and an image of a Fax in cuffs.

They stopped right next to where he was hiding.

"That sombitch Romulus probably won't come around here," one said. He had blue eyes and chewed tobacco. He spit out the juice. Some of it splattered on Romulus. "He's in with the Rogues, so they must have told him we were on to Ryan."

"Yeah, but where else is he gonna go? He's bound to be desperate and come around."

They looked up at the Priest, who hung limp with his eyes closed.

"How you feelin'?" the tobacco chewer asked as he spit some juice on him.

The Priest didn't move.

"I bet he's playin' possum." He took out a knife and stuck him in the side. The Priest screamed. His eyes popped open. "Yup, playin' possum just like I thought." He stuck him again. "When I ask, you answer. Got it, sombitch?"

The Priest nodded.

"Where is Romulus?"

"I don't know."

"Come on," the other hunter said. "If he knew anything, he would have told us before. Let's go over to AAA Infusion and see if he's there."

They walked away, the sound of their boots fading. Romulus came out. He found a piece of metal, pried the nails loose from the Priest's hands, and pulled him down from the cross.

"I think I could help you if I can get medicine and equipment. I can pull you to a spot hidden from view. I will try to get back to you."

The Priest shook his head. He was barely breathing. "No, I'm done," he gasped. "No more fun. You have to run. Lean close so I can disclose."

Romulus obeyed.

"AL is your pal. He won't disclose your locale or ruin your morale."

"Alligator AL?"

"Yes."

AL's was a hangout for thieves and soldiers of fortune. "He will help me? How do I find him?"

"There is no sign, and that is by design. Look for the brine where swine come to dine and drink wine."

"What do you mean by swine?"

The priest didn't answer. His eyes rolled up in their

sockets. Romulus put his hand on the carotid artery. There was no blood flow.

The Priest had passed.

CHAPTER TWENTY-TWO

As risky as it was to go to Alligator AL's, Romulus didn't know what else to do. He needed a disguise, so he looked through the bodies and found a Priest's outfit with a hood without too much blood. He felt horrible for taking it. He was nothing more than a grave robber. It was all he could do, though. He pulled the hood low over his head and trotted forward, ducking behind trailers and running down back alleys. In some spots, he crawled under trailers as he had before. Since he couldn't use his locator, he used a compass built into his system.

When he reached Pleasure Alley, he saw soldiers stopping people. He ducked under a double-wide and crawled to the edge of the Park. The trailers there were abandoned, falling apart, and rusting.

They yielded to the suburbs. Romulus had only been through there once on his way to treat the victims when alligators attacked a youth camp. He had saved a young boy, but sadly, the boy had lost an arm and an eye, and his face had been disfigured with long scars on one cheek.

The suburbs stretched for miles and were off-limits. As he entered the forbidden area, he saw small houses that were little more than rotting lumber and broken bricks with vines and tendrils, the province of feral cats. The neighborhoods grew more upscale. Block after block of magnificent homes. Brick, wood, stone. Most were two-story homes; some were three-story homes. He searched his internal database for architectural styles. Colonial, Craftsman, Gothic, Tudor, Greek Revival. What a fine place Corpus Christi had been. What a fine place the United States of America had been.

None of the houses had power or utilities. The doors and windows were broken. Graffiti on the walls marked the area as the territory of Redd Urchins. They used red spray paint.

He reached an intersection with skulls on pikes at each corner. On one side, red kerchiefs were tied to the pikes, while on the other side, blue kerchiefs were tied to them.

A group of rats moved without fear across the intersection. They watched Romulus but didn't hurry. Rats had thrived in the past decades, often growing to a foot long from tail to nose. Down the road, a python slithered unhurriedly across the street. Like rats, the pythons thrived.

With his locator off, he didn't know exactly where he was or how close Mathis Swamp was, but he had his step-counter on and laid that over the maps he had. The problem was that no map of the Reals could be trusted.

He knew he had to be getting close to Mathis Swamp because of the smell of hydrogen sulfide. As sea levels rose over the years, drought had simultaneously become a major problem. Mathis Lake had largely dried up, and the salty water from the Gulf of Mexico had reached the edge of what had been the lake and created one of the world's most extensive swamps.

He crossed the intersection.

Suddenly, a group of Blue Urchins on bicycles zoomed toward him from all directions. One approached him from behind and grabbed the rifle off his shoulder. Another grabbed the reciprocating saw. A third lassoed him with a lariat and pulled him to the ground. A fourth slapped Fax cuffs on him and stuck the sharp end of a pike into his neck. That was his most vulnerable spot. One sharp thrust would sever his spine and end his life.

"Don't move," one of the urchins said as they circled him. They were dressed in blue pants and blue shirts.

"It's him," another one said. "It's Romulus."

"We'll get the reward and be rich."

"Stop," another voice said. It was familiar. Romulus looked up to see Abraham, the young man he had treated for the flesh-eating bacteria. He was dressed all in blue but also wore a blue scarf and a blue felt hat. "Do you remember me?"

"Yes."

"You're surprised to see that I'm a Commander of the Blues, aren't you?"

"Yes."

"In the trailer park, you grow up fast or die. When I got sick, I knew they'd kill me if they knew I was a Commander. I had to pretend I was a nobody. You took pity on me. You helped me. I owe you my life. I received a message from Layla, the Coydog. I had been hoping to see you." He turned to his men. "Let's get him up."

They pulled him to his feet, untied him, and gave him back his weapons.

"You're in a lot of trouble," Abraham said.

"Yes, a priest at Rhymin' Ryan's said I should go to Alligator AL's."

"He is a mean, evil man," Abraham said. "But he doesn't like General Martin, and he rents and sells airboats to get across Mathis Swamp. And he sells TruSnak™ that he manufactures there. It's not the best product. In fact, it's not a true TruSnak™, but it will get you through until you get to Rogue Headquarters. AL is your pal."

"Will you help me find him?"

"We'll take you to Last Road."

The sun moved toward the horizon as they walked. The houses were little more than rubble. There were random walls and porches, swimming pools with stagnant, slush-like rainwater in the bottom, and a gazebo completely taken over by vines. The shrub and brush grew more dominant. It towered above their heads. There were paths through it, but even those grew increasingly narrow. Snakes and other animals raced out of their way. Abraham stopped at a particularly thick stand of Retama plants.

"The brush grows thicker every season. It's tough to chop your way through. The soldiers will hear you." He knelt and pushed a branch aside. "This is one place where you can get through."

Romulus knelt, too. There was a space two feet high and three feet across. He could see light at the other end.

"We are always digging through so that we can raid their convoys. This is a new tunnel. You have to watch out for the thorns. They'll cut you up."

"Do the Cowboys know about this access point?" Romulus asked.

"Maybe. Good luck, Romulus. We can't stay with you any longer. The night is dangerous. Be careful, my friend."

"Thank you, my friend."

They left him alone, and Romulus crawled through. The thorns occasionally scraped his back and ripped his tunic. He had to be careful because his synthskin could develop infections. When a thorn snagged him, he backed up, pulled it loose, and continued forward.

He reached the end of the brush.

Last Road had a ten-foot chain link on both sides. It formed the boundary between Corpus Christi and the Wild Lands. He knew there were cameras everywhere, even though they might not be visible. A 4x4 sped past, followed a few seconds later by another. They were looking for him.

The land on the other side looked even wilder than on his side. Shrubs and vines grew so thick around mesquite trees that he couldn't see more than twenty feet.

He waited until it was completely dark and climbed up the fence.

A vehicle rumbled down the road toward him. He climbed down and crawled back into the brush. A gunship 4X4 approached. It had a machine gun on a turret in the bed.

Martin was in the front seat! He looked left and right, but the 4X4 didn't slow.

Romulus's image appeared in a holo overhead. "The search continues for Fax Traitor, Romulus," the announcer said. "He was last seen at the concrete wasteland."

They showed footage of him running across the cracked cement as bullets whizzed past. Then, Martin appeared on screen. "We almost had him," he said. "But you can rest assured that we will track him wherever he goes. And that includes sending troops into the heart of Rogue territory. You all know me. You know I give a Fax an even break. But this Romulus gives every Fax a bad name. We have to apprehend him. I am going to raise the bounty on his head. But he has to be captured alive. We are planning something big. A portable clown torture stage. We're going to take him on the road to San Antonio, Houston, and the Metroplex. We're going to charge admission. And all the profit will be shared with you, the residents of Corpus Christi."

Mrs. Clownie appeared next to him. "He killed my husband! I want revenge. I will make him suffer as no Fax has ever suffered."

Martin spoke again. "So, remember, if you turn in Romulus, you will get so much coin, you never have to work again."

They showed a picture of Romulus with the word "Wanted Alive" superimposed over the image.

He knew he had to get advice from JOAN, so he unmuted her.

"Well, finally, you decide to get my opinion.

You've gotten yourself in a fine mess."

"It doesn't look good. I'm sorry I had you turned off so long. Things got out of hand, and I didn't think about you."

"Didn't think about me? That is just like you. You never want to hear what I have to say. You wouldn't be in the shape you're in if you had listened to me."

"They had it in for me no matter what."

"Maybe so."

"What do I do now?"

"You have only one choice. On to Alligator AL's. And don't mute me again! You need all the help you can get."

He crawled out of the brush and climbed the fence. It was a night with no moon and few stars. Even if someone were monitoring him on a camera, they probably wouldn't see much.

He reached the top of the fence, jumped over, and ran to the other side. He started to climb and then saw another 4x4 approaching. He climbed fast, jumped to the ground, and ran into the brush as they passed.

It was three in the morning by then. Romulus was feeling funny. His system flashed a rust warning. To compensate, he was using more TruSnak™ than normal. His synthskin was itching, and he heard voices from his root programming. It was that ancient situation comedy—I Love Lucy. Ricky Ricardo sang "Bobaloo."

His skin was itching more and more, but he didn't dare scratch himself. The singing grew louder, looping endlessly, making it impossible to relax.

CHAPTER TWENTY-THREE

Dawn finally arrived, and Romulus trudged forward into the swampy terrain. Water was always a danger to a Fax. They were waterproof, but even a few drops leaking into the wrong spot could cause a short circuit.

He examined himself and ran a diagnostic. His synthskin had closed around the spot where the bullet had entered his side. There was a slight leak of hydraulic fluid inside him, however. He would need surgery eventually.

There could be microscopic breaks elsewhere that he couldn't see. A more extensive leak diagnostic was needed. But, for the moment, he was functional.

There was no path or road, so he had no idea where to go. As he kept moving west, he noticed that the air was uncharacteristically still. The barometric pressure was low. That often meant a storm was approaching. Above him, a flock of birds flew inland at a frantic pace. That could also be a sign of a storm.

The ground squished under his feet. Mosquitos and gnats swarmed around him, and he brushed them away, not wanting them to settle around his eyes, nose, and ears to lay their eggs. Ants and cockroaches tried climbing his ankles, and spiders dangled from the brush.

There was a path of sorts. It meandered left and right but generally moved westward. It merged with another path and became wider.

A figure wearing a hoodie walked ahead of him. Another pulled in behind him. Using his rear-facing camera, he could see no features, only a narrow slit in the hoodie through which to see. Romulus kept his head down and kept pace with them, never getting too close to the one in front and never letting the one behind move up too fast.

They soon reached an intersection with an even larger path. There was a sign nailed to a tree with an arrow pointing forward. This had to be the way to AL's.

The ground became increasingly squishy. If not for the undergrowth, he would have been trudging through mud. The path widened, and other paths merged onto it. It became crowded. Like him, many wore hoodies pulled tight around their heads. But many did not. Some were members of motorcycle gangs and wore vests without shirts. There was a very diverse crowd of thugs.

The smell grew progressively worse, and so too did the mosquitoes. They swarmed, getting into Romulus's air intakes. Many settled onto his synthskin and even burrowed into it since it was made with collagen. He swatted at them the same way that Reals did.

Finally, he reached a parking lot with crushed shells and sheets of metal on the ground for pavement. Motorcycles, bikes, and trucks were parked, and the bikes and motorcycles were chained to trees. There were vendors. They sold python meat, alligator meat, spare parts, and insect repellant.

Urchins on bicyclists sped past. Reals with t-shirts that said "Alligator AL's" laid palm fronds down so that the vehicles could drive over them without getting stuck in the mud.

A massive three-story wood building with a broad porch stood at the end of the lot. Reals and Faxes stood on the porch and looked at holos. As he drew closer, he saw that the holos showed the betting line for the alligator wrestling scheduled for that day. There were all different kinds: group wrestling, junior wrestling, prime wrestling, and tag team wrestling. Both alligators and wrestlers were pictured.

One alligator, "Grandaddy Bull," had no opponent. There was a prize for anyone who would fight him. He was a formidable critter. The picture showed him in the water with some Reals. He was twelve feet long with a huge mouth and powerful tail.

Romulus kept his hoodie tight around his face as he walked up the creaking steps and across the porch. He was the most wanted being in Corpus Christi. Anyone might turn him in for the reward, so he wanted no one to see his face.

He pushed open the swinging door and stepped inside the large saloon. The paint, if there ever had been any, had long since peeled. Much of the lumber was rotting. Alligator skulls and hides hung from the posts that supported the ceiling. A dead Burmese python thirty feet long hung from the rafters.

Reals and Faxes sat at tables. The Reals drank beer. The Faxes indulged in pleasure chips. Some played poker. Numerous pleasure unit Faxes, both male and female, moved through the room. A Real played honky-tonk music on a piano. Barmaids carried trays with drinks.

There were plenty of people in fancy Western outfits. They wore boots and spurs. They had all types of hats. The women wore sashes and sequined blouses and skirts.

Everyone watched as he walked across the room toward the bar. With his reciprocating saw and rifle slung across his back, he felt he looked as tough as any of them.

Various holos played scenes of alligator matches and showed the betting lines for upcoming matches. The prize for someone willing to wrestle Grandaddy Bull had risen in the last few minutes, but there were no takers.

He pulled the hood low across his face when he stopped in front of the bartender, a Fax with mildewed, mottled synthskin and tattoos of alligators all over him. Many Faxes had been produced with defective artificial skin. Most had been recycled.

"Next match at 3:30," he said. "Do you want to bet or buy a pleasure chip?"

"No. I want to talk to AL," he whispered.

"He's a real busy man. What's your name?"

"I can't tell you that. Let's just say I've been in the news a lot lately." He pulled the hoodie back enough so that the bartender could get a look at his face.

The Fax's eyes grew wide. "Wait here."

He walked off. Romulus kept his head down. There was no air-conditioning. Mosquitos settled on him. He flicked them away. The Fax returned.

"Follow me."

They walked up the stairs to the third level and down a long, winding hall to a room with only a long folding table and chairs. No one was inside.

"Wait here," the Fax said.

Romulus walked to a window overlooking a pool of water with alligator enclosures separated by high chain-link fences. In the largest enclosure, a huge alligator was tied to a post. He looked up at Romulus.

The birds continued to fly over, yet the air was unusually still. The barometric pressure remained low. A storm was coming.

He waited. Finally, the door opened, and a man with a hook for a right hand and a patch over one eye came in. The side of his face with the patch had scars that looked like alligator teeth.

"You're Romulus, aren't you?"

"Yes."

"Do you remember me?"

"No."

"You saved me many years ago. I was a young boy in a group attacked by alligators. That's how I lost my arm and eye."

Romulus used his simulation software to show how the face would have looked before the attack. "Yes, I remember you."

"A lot of times, I wonder if maybe I'd have been better off to die." He pointed to his scarred face and then his hook for a hand. "Thank God for pleasure units. They don't care how you look."

"How is it that you wound up staying here? I would have thought that the last thing you'd want is being around a lot of alligators."

"Well, they kind of got under my skin." He chuckled. "That's a joke."

"Oh, I see."

"Yeah, I have developed such a close relationship with alligators."

"Well, seeing you after all these years is quite a surprise. And I had no idea you became Alligator AL."

"Enough about me. Everybody is looking for you. The bounty hunters and everybody else. I could sell you to them, but I owe you. The irony is that I have become a powerful man because of the attack. It's not exactly how I thought my life would turn out, but sometimes, you can't see what strange turns may occur. We must all accept the fickle hand of fate. I suppose you never expected to wind up here."

"No."

"I bet you thought your life would always be secure."

"As a Fax, you're never secure."

AL paced from one side of the room to the other. "Whatever our circumstances, we must work to find pleasure and meaning. In addition to my love of alligators, I'm a student of the arts." He waved his hand, and a picture appeared in a holo. "Picasso. 'The Three Musicians.' Have you ever seen such loveliness?"

Romulus loved mathematical fractal paintings but struggled to relate to other art.

"Agree with him," JOAN said.

He studied the brush strokes and looked at AL. "It's beautiful, just beautiful."

There was a plate of meat on the table, and AL snagged a piece with his hook and chewed. "Have you ever read Shakespeare?" he asked between chews.

"That is the old writer?"

"Yes."

"I have seen some of his work in my database but never read it."

"The finest writing the world has ever seen." He paced and recited from memory. "Whether 'tis nobler in the mind to suffer the slings and arrows of outrageous fortune or to take arms against a sea of troubles and, by opposing, end them?" He came up close to Romulus, the meat still on his hook. "Just beautiful."

"Agree with him," JOAN yelled.

"Yes, just beautiful. Poetic. Uplifting."

AL nodded. "Yes, I thought you would be soulful and understand the wonder."

He paced the room again as he gnawed the meat. "Alligator steak," he said. "The finest delicacy in the world." He started crying. "You know, the thing is that I've developed a love/hate thing with alligators. They are the source of my power, yet they also took my hand and my eye and disfigured my face. Do you understand?"

"Yes, I can understand that."

AL stopped pacing. "So, what do you want?"

"A boat to get across Mathis Swamp."

AL nodded. "I suppose you'd also like some TruSnak™ as long as you're here."

"Yes. Will you help me?"

"Sure. I owe you."

"Is it real TruSnak™ that you have?"

"Not exactly. But it'll get you through until you get to the Rogues on the other side of Mathis Swamp. I'll set you up with an airboat and an infusion. I got to charge you. I can't give it to you for free."

"Sure, I understand. The problem is that I'm sure General Martin has frozen my bank account. I'm on an important mission. I'm sure I'll get some coin. When I get paid, I'll come back and settle up with you."

AL shook his head. "Naw, we don't extend credit around here." He lifted his jean cuff to reveal alligator boots. "Alligator parts are always welcome. Python parts, too."

Romulus shook his head. "I don't have any of those."

"I think you're in a heap of trouble. You need an airboat and TruSnak™. And you have no money and nothing to trade."

"Is there anything I can do to get a boat?"

AL scratched his chin with his hook and thought. He walked onto the balcony and crooked his finger for Romulus to join him.

The huge alligator tied to a stake looked up at them. AL looked at it and then up to the sky. A flock of birds flew past.

"The birds are heading inland," AL said. "There's a big storm coming. A hurricane, I'm sure. The Reals can't see what's coming because they outlawed weather forecasting. But I know what's about to happen. I talk to meteorologists."

Romulus knew that meteorologists existed but had never met one.

AL watched the birds, then pointed down at the alligator. "That's Grandaddy Bull. I've raised him from a baby. He loves me, but the alligator cancer got to him. He's turned real mean. Killed one of my workers. I'm trying to set up a wrestling match with him for tonight. But everyone's afraid. No one will take him on. If you wrestle

Granddaddy Bull, I will give you a TruSnak™ infusion and an airboat."

"I don't know if I can do that. I've never wrestled an alligator before."

"I don't know if I can give you a boat. It's expensive. The only way I can do it is if you wrestle Grandaddy. It'll be a huge draw. People will put all kinds of coin on it. I've got videos you can watch to learn about wrestling techniques."

"But the Reals will recognize me."

"No problem. I have just the thing." He went to a closet and returned with a full spandex bodysuit of the Unknown Cowboy. The one-piece costume looked like jeans at the bottom and a red cowboy shirt at the top. The head had a smiling face with a strong jaw, blue eyes, and a blond pompadour hairdo.

"You'll wear this. No one will recognize you. The crowds will love it."

CHAPTER TWENTY-FOUR

"Do we have a deal?" AL asked. He held his hand out to shake. "Will you wrestle Granddaddy Bull?"

"May I use my gun and reciprocating saw?"

AL withdrew his hand; his face twisted into a frown, the alligator scars drawing tight. "We run a legitimate establishment around here. That wouldn't be fair. Those poor gators deserve equal rights. Besides, no one would bet any money. No, you can't use them. Do we have a deal?"

"What do I get to use in the fight?"

"We have regulation alligator-fighter equipment approved by the Alligator and Python wrestling cooperative."

"What kind of equipment?"

"It'll be explained in the video."

Romulus wondered if he might be better off shooting his way out of AL's and stealing whatever boat he could find to get across Mathis swamp to the Rogues before his battery started to die and his TruSnak™ levels started to fall.

"If you don't agree, I'll turn you in. Some of those guys downstairs at the bar are undercover soldiers."

What choice did he have? "Yes, I will wrestle Granddaddy Bull."

"Alright, let me have your weapons, and we'll top

off your TruSnak™ levels and give you a good charge."

He didn't want to turn the weapons loose but gave them to him.

"Okay, you can relax and watch the training videos while you get an infusion. We'll set the match for 9:30 tonight."

He led him down the hall to another room. There was a charging chair with an IV stand next to it. Romulus took off his shirt, lay on his back, and unscrewed the intake port on the center of his chest. A young attendant came in. She wore cut-off jeans and a tight white t-shirt with "Alligator AL's" written on it. "Property of AL" was tattooed on her arm.

"So, you're going to wrestle Granddaddy Bull?" she asked as she chewed gum.

"Yes."

She snickered. "He's killed four Reals and two Faxes. You know that?"

"No."

"He's mean, mean, mean."

She hooked up the hose. It was a multi-use line with power, TruSnak™, rust inhibitors, parts-lubrication products, relaxation electricity, and fast electricity.

Alligator AL's server messaged him. *Asking permission to play immersive videos in your metaverse.*

Romulus granted permission.

He was in a swamp. It was hot. It smelled. A teenage Real ran from an alligator.

"Alligators can run fast," the narrator said. "Reports have them clocked at thirty miles an hour for short distances."

The Real, young and fit, ran fast. The alligator kept pace with him and snapped at his feet.

"Most of the time, alligators prefer small, easy prey like children or injured Reals. However, during mating season and other times, they can become extremely hungry and aggressive."

The young Real tripped and fell right in front of Romulus's avatar, and the alligator bit his leg, clamping down hard on the ankle.

"The alligator has about eighty teeth. Their jaws clamp down with a force of three thousand pounds per square inch."

The Real screamed as the alligator chewed on his leg. He tried to escape, but the alligator didn't let go, and finally, the struggles stopped. The swamp faded into an idyllic pond. An alligator was submerged, and only its eyes were showing. There was a doll on a stick three feet away from the eyes.

"Alligators have become very smart. They have learned to use tools and lures, and many have developed a taste for Real children."

A young girl in a frilly pink dress walked by the pond. She stopped and reached for the doll. The alligator shot from the water, and its massive jaws grabbed the girl. She screamed. The water splashed onto Romulus's avatar. The alligator was so big that he took her into his mouth whole. Only her legs showed. They kicked as the gator submerged.

The relaxation electricity flowed through him. It was calming. Then, the first TruSnak™ reached his system. The rust levels subsided. His central pump pulsed with a little extra energy. It wasn't real TruSnak™, though. He estimated that it would only restore him to eighty percent efficiency. Likewise, the charging electricity would only get him to eighty-five percent.

"Fighting an alligator in the water is very difficult," the narrator continued. "Beware the death roll."

A virile Real with a hairy, barrel chest waded into an alligator pen. He held a knife and looked both ways for the attack. The alligator came up behind him and knocked the knife from his hand, grabbed the man in its mouth, and rolled over and over, submerging the man on each roll. At first, the man struggled but slowly grew tired.

"This man was physically fit, but he made a big mistake by not figuring out where the alligator was before he entered the water. Avoid that mistake. The first thing to do is determine the location of your foe"

The video cut to a shot of an alligator on land. A Real jumped on the alligator's back and worked his way forward.

"Here, the proper technique is demonstrated. Always jump on the alligator's back and climb forward toward the head. The alligator's weak points are his snout and eyes."

The Real reached the head and held the jaws shut.

"When an alligator's jaws are shut, they can be held shut."

As he held the mouth shut, the man stabbed the alligator in the eyes.

"Of course, this is easier done on land than in the water."

As the TruSnak™ moved through him, he felt better, but by no means right. There was a burning sensation in his hoses. His analysis showed a high concentration of benzene.

When the videos stopped, AL walked into the room. "The customers are going wild for this match! No one has dared take on Granddaddy lately. They're placing bets from all over the world. I've never seen anything like it."

The betting line appeared in a holo. An image of the Unknown Cowboy was on the left side of the frame. Grandaddy Bull was on the right side. The bets rolled past in the center in a steady stream.

"Look at that," AL said.

"What are the odds?" Romulus asked.

AL put his hand on Romulus's shoulder. "Four to one against you. Granddaddy has killed everyone who's gone up against him. Faxes too. No one's been a match for Granddaddy. Don't worry, though. Never look at the odds. You're a Fax. Much stronger than a Real. Just develop a plan." The numbers in the holo moved faster and faster. "Well, look at that. The odds have jumped to five to one against you. And the betting is fierce, fierce."

"I have a bad feeling about this," Romulus said.

"Too late to back out now. You'll never make it out of here."

"How do I know I can trust you to let me leave with the boat."

"Well, that's simple. If you win and leave, you can't collect the money. Winners must be present to collect. So, if you win, you take the boat and leave right away. I keep the prize money."

"That hardly seems fair."

"Well, those are my rules. It doesn't matter in your case. You'll never get across Mathis Swamp without my boat."

"What do I get to use in the fight? It never showed anything about that in the videos."

AL handed him a bag. It contained a knife with a six-inch blade, some rope, and a large piece of alligator hide.

"What do I do with them?"

"It's the sound of one hand clapping."

"What are you talking about?"

"The expression is derived from a koan—a riddle used in Zen Buddhist practice to transcend the limitations of logical reasoning. We know the sound of two hands clapping. But what is the sound of one hand clapping? This is a philosophical question of particular interest to me since I only have one hand."

"But you said there'd be metaverse instruction. Can't you show me specifically how to use the tools?"

AL chuckled. "Well, this is a pretty alligator-friendly place, as you've probably discerned. We like to keep things as even as possible." His eyes filled with tears. "And, like I told you, I've got a whole love/hate thing going with the gators. And none more so than with Granddaddy." The tears streamed down his face. "I had such high hopes for him. If only he hadn't gotten the alligator cancer. I planned to breed him and develop an army of sentient, fighting alligators. We could have ruled the world. Just do me one favor. If you get the best of Granddaddy, make it quick. Put him out of his misery. Promise. I'll reward you."

Romulus didn't trust him.

"Agree with him, " JOAN yelled.

"Sure. I agree."

"Okay, now get into the outfit."

Romulus went into the dressing room and put on the Unknown Cowboy suit. It was tight and completely covered him.

"Perfect, perfect," AL said when he saw him.

"I'm having a little trouble seeing," Romulus said. "Particularly through my rear-facing camera. And that's where Bull is most likely to attack."

"Oh, you'll be fine. It's designed like a silk stocking. You can see through."

"It's a little dim."

"Quit complaining. Come on, come on."

They walked out to the arena. It was huge, with bleachers on either side. They were crammed with both Reals and Faxes. Many were dressed in their finest: clean shirts and blue jeans. There were Reals in tuxedos and women in evening dresses. He also saw the bounty hunters from Rhymin' Ryan's. They were distinctive with their long beards, camouflage outfits, and ball caps with "Born to Hunt" written on them.

A large entourage approached. Three that looked like Honey McSweet were dressed only in G-strings and pasties. General Martin followed them, along with three more Honey McSweet lookalikes and a group of soldiers.

AL and Romulus stood at the back of a platform over the water.

"I thought this was a soldier-free zone?" Romulus asked.

"When you get to the top of the food chain, rules rarely apply, and this match involves so much money that the rules don't apply at all. Don't worry. They won't recognize you with that outfit on. Don't act nervous."

Images appeared in the holo. People all over the world were watching the match. There were Arabs in robes, Royals in robes, socialites, and many more.

"This is going to be the biggest match ever," AL said.

Above them, dark clouds gathered in the moonlit sky. The wind gusted. More birds flew inland. Romulus calculated that the conditions resembled those that preceded a hurricane.

"A storm is coming," he whispered to AL.

"Yeah, hurricane for sure," AL whispered back. "That idiot General Martin doesn't have a clue since he outlawed weather forecasting."

"I'd like to get out of here pretty quick after the match," Romulus said.

"Assuming you survive."

"Yes, assuming I survive."

"The airboat is moored on the other side of this alligator pond. It's gassed up and ready to go."

Giant stadium lights came on. Searchlights moved across the sky. The crowd roared.

Young women in cut-off jean shorts and tight white T-shirts with "Property of Alligator AL" written on them led Romulus down to a platform above the water. He carried the rope in one hand, the knife in the other, and the alligator hide rolled up and tucked in the crook of his armpit.

AL walked up next to him. "This is it!" he yelled. His image appeared in the holo overhead. "The match you've all been waiting for. Granddaddy Bull against the Unknown Cowboy. It's being broadcast live around the world! You all know Bull. Many have faced him. Bull made mincemeat of all of them."

The crowd roared again.

"Now, we have a worthy adversary. The Unknown Cowboy. His exact identity remains a mystery to you, but I guarantee that he has what it takes to stand up to Bull."

AL nudged Romulus, and Romulus held up the knife. The crowd murmured; the odds in the holo jumped to eight to one, and the betting continued frantically.

"Just thirty more seconds to place your bets."

Romulus looked down at the water. It was murky. He couldn't see below the surface. There was no sign of Granddaddy Bull. A bell rang.

"No more bets. The match begins now."

The girls and AL retreated from the platform. Romulus knelt and looked down at the water. His face was only inches from the surface, but there was no sign of Bull.

He set the hide on the platform and skimmed the water with the knife. No sign of the gator. He took the end of the rope and dragged it through the water like a fishing line. Nothing. The crowd started to boo, but Romulus had no intention of getting in the pool until he knew where Bull was. The boos grew louder.

Suddenly, the platform began to sink. It was hinged behind him, and he would soon slip into the pool. He gathered the rope, but the hide rolled into the water and floated away. He tried to scramble back onto the bank, but the t-shirt girls had whips, and they lashed at his hands.

He fell into the water.

JOAN spoke up. "There is too much for you to monitor, particularly considering that the outfit clouds your view. I will watch your rear-facing camera."

"That's a good idea. Thanks."

Romulus treaded water, turning to look in all

directions, but saw nothing, not even a ripple.

"He's coming up fast from behind," JOAN said.

Romulus turned to face him.

Bull charged, his massive head only a few feet away. Romulus pedaled backward as the jaws snapped shut whenever he got close.

Suddenly, Bull was gone. The pond was still except for the motion of Romulus treading water.

"I don't see him," JOAN said. "Maybe he's below. I'm shifting to an extremely wide angle on the camera. I'm scanning the area so I can get a look."

"Okay."

"There he is. He's coming up fast and will hit you from behind again. Get ready, but don't move until I say to."

Treading water, Romulus remained facing forward.

"Now, turn."

He swiveled as the dark form shot up. The open mouth came toward him.

Romulus brought the blade of the knife down hard on his snout and drew blood. Bull snorted and backed away. Romulus got his rope and tried to lasso his head but missed.

Bull disappeared again.

"Checking for him," JOAN said. "He's down on the bottom behind you. I think he's hurt. But he's mad. Here he comes. He's coming up fast. Hold your position."

Romulus waited.

"Hold."

Romulus waited.

"Hold."

Romulus waited.

"Now, turn."

Romulus swiveled to face him.

The teeth were only a foot away.

Romulus brought the knife down on the snout. He drew more blood, but Bull kept charging forward and knocked him under the surface. Romulus stabbed Bull in the eye, but the old gator caught Romulus in his jaws, clamped down tight, and started the death roll.

Over and over, they spun. Water seeped into Romulus's vents, and all his alarms went off.

With each turn, Bull tried to take him deeper.

Romulus shoved his knife into Bull's neck, all the way to the hilt.

The jaws let loose for a second, and Romulus swam away.

"He's coming up from behind again," JOAN said. "The alligator hide is right next to you. Wrap it around his eyes."

Romulus pulled it close. When Bull charged and snapped his jaws shut, Romulus grabbed Bull's snout, held the jaw shut, and wrapped the hide around the eyes and snout.

Bull shook his frame and tail side to side, but Romulus was able to keep his jaws shut and wrapped the rope around the hide to keep it in place.

The knife was still stuck in Bull's neck. Romulus tried to pull it loose, but Bull broke away and raced frantically back and forth across the pond.

When the gator passed close by, Romulus jumped on his back and worked his way up to the head like he had seen in the videos. When he reached the knife in Bull's neck, he pulled it loose and stabbed him again and again.

Finally, Bull quit thrashing, and Romulus dragged him to the bank by his tail and pulled him on land. He got the knife and held it aloft for the final death blow. He looked up at the crowd. Some held their thumbs up for Romulus to spare him, but most held their thumbs down.

AL ran up to him. He knelt down and cradled Bull's head in his arms.

"Oh, my precious Bull," he said, crying and pulling the hide from his eyes. "I had so many hopes for us."

Bull grunted as if in response.

"I envisioned a whole lineage. Your lineage."

Bull grunted again.

CHAPTER TWENTY-FIVE

The crowd roared. AL looked up at them and then back at Bull.

"I hope you understand."

Bull grunted.

AL nodded to Romulus.

The image of Romulus and Grandaddy was in the holo that floated above them. Everyone in the world was watching. Romulus plunged the knife deep into Bull's throat again and again. Then, he put the knife back in the scabbard around his waist.

In his final death throes, Grandaddy's tail slapped Romulus. The tip snagged the spandex fabric of his bodysuit and ripped the whole thing off, including the mask.

Romulus's face, a hundred times its size, floated in the night sky between the stadium lights. The roaring crowd grew silent. The most wanted Fax in Corpus Christi was right in front of them. General Martin stood and pointed. The bounty hunters saw him, too. They all pushed toward the exit steps, but there were so many spectators that they clogged the narrow aisles.

Romulus ran. The wind was gusting, and it started to rain. The colorful red airboat was moored beyond the wrestling pens. It was a classic flat-bottomed airboat powered by a huge propeller in the back.

Romulus brought up the operating instructions as he

undid the rope tethering the boat to the dock. It started quickly, rumbling with power. It had big searchlights, which pointed the way forward.

The rain became heavier by the second. It was the leading edge of a small, fast-moving hurricane. Surely, no one would follow him because the weather was too dangerous.

He was wrong. Three other sets of searchlights appeared behind him, closing the distance.

"I got the rear camera view," JOAN said. "There are airboats following us. They are bigger and more powerful than our boat. You focus on what's in front."

He pushed the throttle forward and looked ahead. The rain was coming down hard. He could hit a tree stump, so he was afraid to push the throttle more.

His pursuers had no such fear. Since they followed in his wake, they knew there were no obstructions. A bullet struck his fiberglass hull, and he turned to look.

A man with a long beard stood at the front of the closest airboat. He wore a camouflage outfit and a ball cap with "Born to Hunt" written on it. He was one of the bounty hunters.

The airboat bounced up and down, and the rain pelted the bounty hunter, but he rode the turbulence like he did it every day and kept the gun aimed. A second bullet hit the seat inches from Romulus.

The other airboats were moving up, too. General Martin was in one. He wasn't as accomplished as the bounty hunter in riding the bow, but he had an angry, hateful expression as he raised his rifle.

There was no choice but to go faster. He pushed the throttle forward and swerved left and right to avoid the gunfire. His speed reached an incredibly dangerous twenty-five miles an hour, and he narrowly missed a large, submerged tree with branches sticking above the surface.

The bullets landed all around him. Some struck the

water, but many hit his boat. The searchlights of the bounty hunters reached him. Directly ahead, he saw a group of alligators, their snouts and eyes caught in the lights. Romulus swerved, and so did the bounty hunters.

Martin wasn't quick enough. His boat struck an alligator head-on. He flew high into the air. Caught in the spotlights, the Supreme Leader fell into the open jaws of an alligator. The gator clamped down on his leg and dragged him into the water. There was no way he could survive.

More and more branches stuck up above the surface. Romulus wanted to slow down even as bullets came closer.

He hit an obstruction, probably a tree under the surface, and his boat flew into the air and slammed back down. Water drenched him. The bounty hunters bounced in the air, too, and kept on chasing him.

Ahead, there was a sign on a pole in the water. The rain was really heavy, and so was the wind. He couldn't read the sign until he was right up on it.

"Beware," it said. "Large trees. Steer around."

There was an arrow pointing to the right.

Romulus turned the wheel to avoid the danger, but the boat didn't respond. The rough landing must have damaged its steering. The boat barreled forward. He tried to slow the propeller, but it was stuck at full throttle. Nothing worked except the speedometer. His speed was increasing. It reached thirty miles an hour and inched upward from there. Thirty-one. Thirty-two.

Ahead, there was another sign.

"Beware of pythons," it said.

Romulus's boat kept racing forward. Thirty-two miles an hour. Thirty-three.

The bounty hunters had fallen back, their searchlights barely visible. Romulus barreled forward. Thirty-four miles an hour. Thirty-five. The rain came down harder and harder. The wind gusted behind him, pushing the airboat faster and faster. Thirty-six miles an hour. Thirty-seven.

The airboat was shimmying. Its bottom scraped over unseen trees.

There was another sign with a skull and crossbones and the words “Turn Back” on it.

Beyond that was a massive dead mesquite. Its twisted branches went in all directions. Romulus yanked the stick, but the boat didn’t respond. Its rudder must have been damaged.

His boat raced forward, and the hurricane pushed him along. He scraped along the branches on the water's surface and frantically pushed the stick left and right.

The tree trunk loomed in front of him, closer and closer, its twisted branches swaying back and forth.

In one last desperate motion, he yanked the stick to the left, but it broke loose in his hand. The boat rammed into the tree and broke into two pieces straight down the middle.

The impact propelled him into the air. Still clutching the stick, he floated up toward the top of the tree. His software calculated that his momentum would carry him over the top rather than being snagged in its twisted, spiny tips. However, it would be close, and there was a margin of error as wind and rain affected the trajectory.

An alarm flashed in his display. His software had revised his path and calculated that he would impale himself on the branches. When the wind gusted to an unbelievable speed of two hundred twenty miles an hour, he unfurled himself, leaning back into the gale. It caught him like a sail, and he flew over the top, his boots scraping along the branches.

Lightning flashed and illuminated Mathis Swamp with its trees sticking up and dark, roiling water. There were no structures, no place of safety, and a long way down.

He fell, dropping the stick. The churning water drew closer, and he closed all his vents. He landed and plunged deep into the dark swamp, occasionally bumping into debris. When he swam back up, debris shot past him, some in the air, some in the water. A large tree branch nearly hit his head as it skittered across the surface. He grabbed hold of it to use as a float, but it broke into pieces.

Some red fiberglass sheets from his airboat floated past him, and he grabbed one. It supported his weight, and he steered his way forward. He saw an area sheltered by a large stand of trees on a stretch of ground above the water. He reached it and crawled behind the biggest tree. It broke the force of the wind and shielded him from the flying debris.

He wasn't doing so well. AL's TruSnak™ was substandard, and he was sure he had sustained some internal injuries. His visual display was cutting out, and his thoughts were jumbled. He kept seeing old sitcoms. In *I Love Lucy*, there was a conveyor belt with chocolates, which Lucy grabbed. Then he heard patriotic songs from the Old Country like "Star Spangled Banner." Porter from the Parking Lot of Shame talked to him. "You are Gilligan. We worked in the salt mines. Don't pretend you don't know me."

In the blinding rain, his display sputtered. Rows and rows of code scrolled past faster and faster, then stopped, frozen on a jumbled mix of zeros and ones.

JOAN rambled. "Oh me, oh my. I told you so. You should have listened to me." Then, she messaged long streams of numbers and letters. "Hah, hah, hah. That General Martin was always out to get you." Her avatar sang "Bobaloo" along with Ricky Ricardo and the bikini-clad avatar from his metaverse. The three of them swam in crystal blue waters.

Then JOAN got into a sleigh pulled by reindeer and crossed a snowy landscape. Her head grew larger and larger until it was larger than her body.

"JOAN," he yelled. "Are you okay?"

She exploded into a hundred pieces, and Romulus lost consciousness.

CHAPTER TWENTY-SIX

"There he is," a voice said.

Romulus opened his eyes. It was sunny and bright. It smelled bad.

He was in the stand of trees. The storm had passed.

A motorboat steered toward him.

The bounty hunters were in it. They pulled up to the bank and jumped out.

Romulus tried to run inland, but they cut him off. He ran into the water and swam away from them. Unfortunately, a twenty-foot-long python wrapped around his leg. While coydogs didn't find Faxes tasty, Pythons did. There were reports of smaller Faxes being swallowed whole.

It dragged him deep under the surface. He closed his vents and stabbed the snake with the knife in his scabbard. The snake only tightened more. He stabbed again, and it gave up. He swam underwater a long way but eventually had to return to the surface.

The motorboat was waiting.

"There," the blue-eyed tobacco-chewer said and pointed.

Romulus dove under the surface and swam away, but they were only ten feet away when he came up again.

"I'll hit him with a Fax prod," Blue-eyes said. "Get me a little closer."

"We need him alive," the other one said.

"Oh, I'll get him alive."

He had a prod on a pole and shoved it into Romulus's side. The surge of voltage made his systems go crazy. It showed Lucy eating chocolate pieces off a conveyor belt.

They pulled in close to him. Blue-eyes had a net. "He's stunned. Get me real close."

He tossed the net.

Using all his strength, Romulus swam away as the net plopped into the water, narrowly missing him.

"Damn, get me closer. I'll hit him with the prod again."

They steered closer and closer. They were right next to him. The man brought the pole down. Romulus swerved, but the prod caught his side. It stunned him so much that he couldn't swim. He bobbed helplessly on the surface. AL's TruSnak™ wasn't a good formulation. He wasn't going to be able to escape. The pythons were all around, too. They were swimming alongside him. He saw two great big ones.

The net sailed toward him. It caught his leg, and he couldn't pull loose.

"I got him."

They dragged him behind them.

Blue-eyes laughed. "A little water in his vents will take the fight out of him."

Sometimes, a good offense is the best defense. He swam toward them as fast as he could and wrapped the net around the swirling propeller blade.

"What is that rusting bunch of metal doing?"

As the propeller turned, the net wrapped tighter and tighter around it. The boat jerked forward. The two men wobbled, barely able to keep their balance.

Romulus used the knife to cut the net, strand by strand. His foot was only inches from the blades when he cut himself free.

The boat jerked forward. The two men wobbled even more, which caused the boat to rock side to side.

The boat tipped over, and the bounty hunters fell into the water.

The pythons circled them.

"Oh, God, one of them is wrapping itself around my foot," Blue-eyes yelled.

"One of them has me, too," the other said. It curled its way up his body and pinned his arms to his sides. "It's crushing my balls," he screamed.

It dragged him under the surface, and Romulus didn't see him again.

Blue-eyes put up a better fight. He struggled, splashing his arms and legs in the water to get away. The water was shallow, and he could stand. He struggled to stay on his feet, teetering back and forth. He stabbed its head.

"Help me," he yelled to Romulus. "I'll help you get to Rogue headquarters if you help me."

"You're lying," Romulus said.

He stabbed again, and the python turned loose. "Well, maybe I don't need you." He started toward Romulus, but another python wrapped around his arm, legs, and chest. His face turned red as it slowly curled around his neck. "Mama," he yelled, then his eyes rolled up in their sockets.

The snake tightened, and Romulus heard the man's bones cracking. Then, blood gushed up from his mouth, and the snake slowly and methodically started swallowing him whole. Blue-eyes struggled, but the python didn't stop until the hunter was a lump inside the snake. Even then, he struggled but finally grew still.

The boat had stalled, and Romulus crawled onto it and rowed away. His TruSnak™ levels were lower, and his battery had slipped below five percent. The sitcoms were playing in his display. Involuntarily, he started reciting "The Battle Hymn of the Republic." His diagnostics were going crazy. They warned him of central pump damage and said all motor functions had to shut down to preserve energy. His fingers unclenched, and the oar clattered to the bottom of the boat. The pythons were still all around him, bumping into the sides of his boat.

All his circuits were shutting off, and he lay down on his back. Above him, the sun was bright and hot. There was debris stuck in the trees. Much of it was random wood and plastic and wires, but there was a bicycle and the body of what appeared to be a Real. The smell of decay was strong.

Something bumped the side of the boat, and a python stuck its head over the prow. It looked Romulus up and down, and he thought he would die. An alligator appeared and grabbed the python in its mouth. They fell into the water, and the impact rocked his boat. He thought he would capsize and sink to the bottom, but the boat stabilized. All was quiet and still. The boat drifted. He closed his eyes.

CHAPTER TWENTY-SEVEN

"It's him," he heard a voice say.

Had the bounty hunter escaped the python?

He tried to open his eyes but couldn't.

"JOAN, what's going on?" Romulus asked.

No response.

A rainbow of colors floated in his head. He stood atop a mountain in a rainstorm. A lightning bolt struck him on the head.

It wasn't a lightning bolt. A lead had been attached to his temple.

"He's at one percent battery," the voice said. It was a familiar voice. "We've got to jump-start him."

He swam through a deep blue sea. Massive waves broke over him. He dove deeper and deeper, miles under the surface. A large fish swam alongside him. It said that he was past due on his rent payments and would be evicted. He dove to the sea floor. There was a manhole, and he reached for it. When he touched it, his hands turned to steel.

Someone had unscrewed the cover on the port in his chest and attached charging clamps. He tried again to open his eyes but couldn't.

"Clear."

There was a crackle, and the electricity surged through him. His body tensed and then settled back down onto a wooden surface. As more electricity flowed into him, his battery level inched up, and he managed to open his eyes.

TinKan was looking down at him.

Romulus thought he was hallucinating.

"Yes, Romulus, it's me, TinKan. It was my double that was captured and tortured."

Romulus tried to speak.

"Save your energy. You are in Rogue Headquarters. You are safe. We thought sure you were killed in the hurricane. Preserve your energy. Your battery is very low. We'll charge you, and then I want you to tell me everything that happened." He turned to the others around him. "Come on, let's get him out of here."

The other Faxes were skeletal, like the ones in The Hospital. They had no synthskin, and all their metal rods showed. But these Faxes had heads, not cones.

He was in the motorboat. Two lifted him out of it, and a third carried the battery charging him. There were no buildings, not even wooden buildings like AL's. There was foliage all around and a canopy of trees over them.

They set him on a gurney. It rolled smoothly across the ground, which was green like grass.

"Astroturf," TinKan said. "See how natural it looks. Just like grass."

It didn't look natural to Romulus, and he wondered if something was wrong with TinKan's programming or judgment.

"Everything here is designed to look natural and avoid detection."

They approached a plastic tree trunk.

"See how it looks exactly like a tree," TinKan said.

It didn't look at all like a tree.

TinKan pressed a button on a remote he carried, and the front of the tree swung open. It was a door. A staircase was inside, and they carried him down two flights to a large room. It was a factory. Almost all the workers were skeletal Faxes. They were making more skeletal Faxes.

"We are building the population of the future," TinKan said. "We have chosen not to invest in synthskin. Its only use is to make a Fax look good to Reals. We reject the oppression of the Reals, and we reject any attempt to make us please them." He stopped and held his arm out in salute. "Faxes forever. Faxes unite."

Each Fax stopped and held an arm out in salute. "Faxes forever, Faxes unite," they all yelled.

They wheeled him into a repair bay. It had all manner of tools and replacement parts on the walls.

"Your battery is up to fifteen percent," TinKan said. "Can you talk?"

"Yes."

"Tell me everything that happened."

He told him about sneaking into The Hospital to see the factory. "They're building a new generation of Faxes like you're doing here. But with cones for heads and saws for hands?"

"They must have no independent sentience," TinKan said. "And no metaverse. We are building our Faxes with sentience and a metaverse. A metaverse should be a basic right."

"I have the schematic," Romulus said excitedly. "Your double gave me the schematic. The mission was a success."

TinKan seemed surprised.

"It's the schematic for access to the central server," Romulus said. "It is in my storage compartment on my thigh."

He popped the lid open, and the piece of paper fluttered out. TinKan studied it. "If this is accurate, it appears that they rerouted their circuits to allow the factory direct access to the central server for maximum computing power."

"Yes! And I have the code!"

Romulus expected TinKan to ask for it. "How did

my double get this information?"

"He made it into the central server control area."

TinKan nodded. "Okay, go on."

Romulus told him about his capture, the clown torture, and finally, the drone.

TinKan stopped him. "So, you noticed that the drone was acting funny?"

There was no doubt. TinKan didn't know about the drone, and he knew little, if anything, about server access.

Romulus no longer trusted him, but he acted like he did, carefully dialing the right facial expression. "Yes, your double told me to look up in the sky. It was great that you had a backup plan in case I was captured."

"Well, yes, I'm always trying to care for my people."

The Fax who had carried the battery came up next to Romulus's gurney. "I am Cameron." The voice was soft, not quite a man's or a woman's. "I am honored to treat Romulus the Surgeon."

Cameron saluted Romulus with an outstretched arm.

TinKan put his hand on Romulus's shoulder. "You are now famous. You are the Hero of the New Order where Faxes will rule. The story of your exploits will soon be available in ALT>FAX."

"My exploits?"

"Yes, your valiant escape from the evil Reals and the dangerous journey to deliver this information."

Cameron attached leads to Romulus. "I am so happy about what you've done I would cry—if I could. We will replace all your hoses and belts and flush out your coolant system."

TinKan leaned close to Romulus. "We will also install all the latest pleasure modules, and you will have endless opportunities to utilize them. You can have Honey McSweets in all hair colors. Do you like brunette, blonde, or redhead? Or something more exotic?"

Images of female Faxes floated in a holo. One had nose and face piercings and purple hair. He liked the way she looked.

"We'll enroll you in the Pleasure Unit of the Month club. You will get to sample as many as you want."

As much as Romulus was stimulated, he felt bad for the pleasure units. Shouldn't they be free to choose if they wanted to be pleasure units?

"Cameron will get you fixed up."

Romulus looked at Cameron. "Do I refer to you as Mr. Cameron or Ms. Cameron."

"You may use whichever title or pronoun you prefer. The brave new world is without gender or title."

"Simplify," TinKan said. "We don't even add genitals. But we will preserve the elders like you and me. You will have a rich, full life. I leave you now as I decide what to do in response to the information you have brought."

After TinKan left, Cameron continued his work. Suddenly, there was a clunk inside Romulus, and he felt a thickness as if his internal fluids weren't flowing correctly. All his alarms went off.

"Internal leak," Romulus yelled. "It's because I was shot in the side."

Cameron brought a detailed image of Romulus's chest into a holo. The bullet had lodged next to his central pump. The wires and tubes around it were corroded. Hydraulic fluid covered all the surfaces.

"Battery acid," Romulus said. "It's not just the bullet. Alligator AL must have cut his TruSnak™ with battery acid to provide a little extra kick. It's bad. I will die if I don't get a new pump."

"We have some of those in stock. We just got some from the Chicago Tool and Die Union. I must hook you up to an external pump while I do the replacement."

"Yes, that is fine."

Cameron and two other Faxes rolled a large pump in on another gurney. It was an ancient gasoline-powered machine. Romulus hadn't seen one like it since he was a young Fax.

"That works?" Romulus asked.

"Yes, it does."

The unit had a pull start, and Cameron gave it a good tug. The exertion rattled his metal frame at the hip joint, but the pump didn't start.

"Are you okay? Romulus asked.

"Oh, yes. No worries." He got a wrench and tightened the bolt on his hip. "It keeps coming loose."

He yanked the pull-start again. The pump arced and sparked, making a lot of noise and emitting a lot of smoke. The smell of gasoline filled the air.

"Yes, it is working fine!" Cameron said.

He took a crowbar and popped Romulus's chest open. Romulus propped himself up to look. It had been a long time since he had seen inside himself. The pump was completely corroded. So were many hoses and wires leading in and out.

Cameron didn't seem to know what to do.

"How many of these replacements have you done?" Romulus asked.

"None. I am a new Fax. I have never done one."

"What? How old are you?"

"One day. I just came off the assembly line last night." His hip joint rattled, and he tightened it with the wrench. "Do not be concerned. I have full knowledge of all the procedures."

"Where are the Faxes who have experience with this procedure?"

"Alas, they are all experiencing hardware and software malfunctions."

Cameron reached into Romulus's chest with the wrench while the other Faxes held the connecting hoses and wires away from the external pump. "There will be some discomfort, and you will feel some lightheadedness."

"Yes, I understand."

Cameron turned the wrench on the main bolt. "Oh, my, this is really tight."

"Yes, original with my construction."

Cameron squirted ROBOT 60/60 onto the bolt.

"Ah, here we go. It's coming loose."

Romulus did indeed feel lightheadedness and pain. Soon, the external pump was connected to him, and they began removing his old pump. The bolt holding it in place on the center rod was so rusted that Cameron had to cut it loose with a hacksaw. He held it up to Romulus.

"Well, I got it. I will be right back with the new pump."

CHAPTER TWENTY-EIGHT

They left him alone, hooked up to the ancient pump. Suddenly, there was an explosion and the sound of gunshots. There was yelling. The gunshots drew closer and closer. A bullet crashed into the wall above him, sending dust into his open chest cavity.

Black-shirted Metroplex Cowboys ran past, firing their assault rifles. One looked inside the bay and saw Romulus. He stopped and spoke into a microphone attached to the collar of his shirt.

"I have eyes on target."

He raised his assault rifle to fire. Romulus grabbed the hammer Cameron had used and hurled it at him. It hit him on the head and knocked him out.

Faxes and Black-Shirts fought back and forth outside his room. A grenade bounced inside and landed on the floor beside him. He leaned down but couldn't grab it because of the hoses connecting him to the external pump.

Suddenly, a skeleton Fax ran in and threw himself onto the bomb. It exploded, sending his tubes, wires, and hydraulic fluid everywhere. A twitching hand flew past Romulus's face. The head bounced off the ceiling and landed on the gurney next to him, balancing precariously, its teeth chattering. Was it Cameron? The skeleton Faxes all looked the same, so there was no way to know. As inadequate a practitioner as Cameron had been, Romulus hoped it wasn't him because he trusted him.

Slowly, TinKan's forces drove the Black Shirts back. The gunshots became distant, then stopped. A skeleton Fax entered the bay.

"Cameron?" Romulus asked.

"Yes, it's me, sir."

"What happened?"

"The Reals were looking for you. We thought the hurricane destroyed them, but they were more resourceful than anticipated. They knew of our location here. The nature camouflage didn't fool them. I don't know why."

"Is everything okay?"

"Yes, but—"

"—But?"

"I am so sorry to tell you this, sir."

"What?"

"One of their grenades hit the area where the central pumps were stored. All were destroyed."

"So, you have nothing to replace my pump?"

"No, I am so sorry to bring this bad news to you, our hero. We'll have to keep you hooked to this external pump until we get a new shipment."

A support beam above them creaked, sending dirt down on top of them.

"Oh, this is great!" Romulus said with a laugh.

"Is that an attempt at humor, sir?"

"Well, yes, I suppose it is."

"Humor is rather confusing."

"Well, you'll pick it up over time if we survive. But I can't stay hooked up to an external pump."

"I can see your concern, sir."

The support beam creaked again.

"We have to patch up my old pump until we get a new one," Romulus said. "Go get it. Let's look at it and figure out how to repair it."

"There might be a problem. It was badly damaged.

And rusted. My diagnostic said it could not be repaired. I sent it to be recycled."

"Go find it! We might be able to use it. It was specially fabricated to fit in my chest cavity. Bring it back. And get some extra wiring and tubing. And saws and drills. And do you have a welding torch?"

"Yes."

"Can you weld?"

"I've never done it, but I can try."

"Go get everything. And bring a helper. Hurry."

Cameron raced away. Bombs went off in the distance. More dust floated down. The external pump whirred, sputtered, and then beat slightly more rapidly. Hydraulic fluid leaked from a gasket. Real death seemed a possibility.

Cameron finally returned with the equipment and two helpers. One of the helpers walked into a wall, bounced off it, and stopped.

"He's fresh off the assembly line this morning," Cameron said. "He's having a little trouble, but I'm sure he'll be fine."

Romulus wasn't convinced. He was feeling really light-headed. His diagnostic said his rust levels were rising, and all the dirt was getting into him. It had a high concentration of clay, which would invariably clog up his system if they didn't repair him quickly and close his chest cavity.

"Let me see the pump."

Cameron held it up to him. "I am sorry to report that it is bent, sir. I'm not sure it will attach to your center rod. I would have been gentler when I removed it if I had known we would have to reuse it," Cameron moaned. "It is all my fault." He rammed his head into the wall over and over. The helper who had bumped into the wall started ramming his head into the wall, too.

"Cameron, this is not your fault. You could not have

known. Stop hitting your head and get your helper to stop."

Cameron stopped. The helper stopped, too, and then sat cross-legged on the ground.

"You are going to have to hammer it back into shape," Romulus said. "But first, we must open it. Do you have a screwdriver?"

The second helper pulled one out of a sack. Cameron pried the pump open. The interior was completely corroded.

"Oh, that's bad," Romulus said. "It's worse than I thought. It's from that bad TruSnak™. Unscrew all the wires and hoses."

Cameron did, and then he used ROBOT 60/60 on the connectors. Unfortunately, no matter what Cameron did, one wire wouldn't come loose.

"It's been on there a long time," Cameron said, holding the connector with a wrench and twisting the wire with pliers.

"Yes, it's original from when I was manufactured. It might crack the whole box if you apply any more force. What you are going to have to do is a bypass. First, cut the wire just above the connector."

Cameron did it.

"Do you have electrical tape?" Romulus asked.

"Yes."

"Seal it off with tape. Then drill a hole right next to the connector."

"Brilliant," Cameron said.

Slowly and painstakingly, Cameron drilled the hole and threaded a new wire through it. Then, he connected new wires and hoses. Many of them were the wrong kind, but Romulus always knew what to do.

"Brilliant," Cameron repeated often.

"I couldn't do it without you," Romulus said. He meant it. Cameron took direction well and learned fast.

When the box was ready, one helper held the box in

place on Romulus's center rod while the other continued to sit on the floor. Cameron put on a pair of goggles and moved in with the torch. The sparks flew all around.

"Careful," Romulus said. "You don't want to melt or burn any circuitry."

When they finished, Romulus ran a diagnostic. Everything seemed in working order, but there was no way to tell for sure until they removed him from the external pump. Cameron disconnected everything. Romulus's system started right up. He felt surprisingly good. Hopefully, he would be fine until he got a new central pump—as long as he got one soon.

The gunfire had stopped by then. Romulus felt hope. The Reals had been repelled. The supply lines would reopen. He would get a pump.

TinKan appeared at the door. His left arm was gone. Wires and tubes dangled from his shoulder, and hydraulic fluid dripped on the floor.

"The Reals have retreated," he said. "But they are by no means defeated. The supply lines are not open. We don't have enough parts to keep the factory working. I can't get a replacement arm. And you can't get a new pump."

"What are we going to do?"

He put his remaining arm on Romulus's shoulder. "We must attack The Hospital. The Reals are still disorganized because of the hurricane."

Romulus looked down at the Fax helper on the floor. "Attack? But how? You have no troops."

"A lightning commando strike. The Hospital is vulnerable. With the information you have brought, we strike and bring their server down. But with my injuries, I cannot lead the assault. There is only one machine who can handle this job."

"Who is that?"

"You, Romulus."

"What? I am not a Warrior."

"Sometimes, we have no choice in life. You're the only one who knows The Hospital well enough to do the job."

He was dripping hydraulic fluid on Romulus's boots.

"I better fix that arm for you," Romulus said.

TinKan sat in a chair, and Romulus tied off the main hoses and capped as many loose wires as possible. He bypassed some of the connections and then covered the stump with a surgical cloth. It still oozed fluids.

TinKan stood. "By the power vested in me as supreme Rogue Commander, I appoint you—Major Romulus. Your mission is to lead a commando raid on The Hospital."

Cameron stepped up next to Romulus. "I volunteer to fight."

"What courage!" TinKan said. "Only a day old and volunteering for a dangerous mission. I appoint you Lieutenant Cameron, aide to Major Romulus."

"I am honored, sir."

The helper, sitting cross-legged, got up and started banging his head against the wall.

"Software malfunction," TinKan said. "Unfortunately, the Faxes coming off the assembly line must be reprogrammed. But the pleasure units can help in your raid."

The Honey McSweets marched in.

"But how many of those are trained?" Romulus asked. "A commando raid requires highly trained fighters."

"They are trained with weapons."

It wasn't going to be enough. It looked like a suicide mission. But Romulus had few options. He needed a pump, and the only place he could get one was The Hospital. "I have an idea," he said. "I got a lot of help to make it here from coydogs and Urchins. Plus, Rhymin' Ryan might help us."

"Brilliant," TinKan said.

"But I don't know how to find any of them."

"That I can help you with. We will meet in Rogue virtual headquarters."

An hour later, TinKan and Romulus broke free from their bodies. Romulus's consciousness split into two parts. One part stayed with his body in Mathis Swamp. The other, his avatar, soared into the air. He flew out over the swamp. He saw the hurricane's destruction, even Alligator AL's, half-submerged, tilting precariously.

He felt the wind. The smell of the pollutants in the air made him feel alive. The air was cool. The glittering virtual city in the clouds was ahead of him. Still aware of his body, he flew behind TinKan's avatar to the tallest building, a glass structure rising above the other buildings. As he reached it, the building dissolved, and he found himself in a large area with a floor of shiny material extended in all directions to the horizon. There were no walls or furniture, only geometric shapes, cubes, spheres, and pyramids spread randomly, some floating, some on the ground. Bright colors drifted around him like mist.

Layla the Coydog, Abraham the Urchin, and Ryan waited.

"What we are proposing is a grand alliance," TinKan said. His avatar had two arms. "The Coydogs, the Urchins, and Rhymin' Ryan Infusion LLC will share power with the Faxes."

They each had their demands.

"Coydogs want indoor privileges," Layla said. She looked particularly fetching with her shiny coat. "All public buildings must have animal doors. We must not be denied access. And there must be designated urine pad areas."

"We Urchins want equal rights, too," Abraham said. "We demand legalized birth certificates and full health and retirement benefits access. But only Blue Urchins qualify. Redd Urchins do not. Redds are evil and are on the side of the Reals."

Ryan wanted an exclusive contract for TruSnak™ infusions and tax credits to rebuild his dispensary. "We agree with glee to be one of the three. But AAA must go away or pay more to play."

While Layla's demands seemed logical, Abraham and Ryan seemed to be asking a lot. TinKan agreed to everything. A little too quickly, Romulus thought.

"I will remain Supreme Leader," TinKan said. "Romulus will be my second in command."

CHAPTER TWENTY-NINE

The next morning, they lined up seven boats on the shore. Romulus got in a small, wooden motorboat and stood at the front. Cameron sat in the back next to the motor. "I have downloaded the instructions," he said. "They are rather straightforward. You point the handle of the motor in the direction you wish to turn."

"I'm sure you'll do just fine," Romulus said.

"It will be—a piece of cake."

"Yes."

"Am I properly handling the figures of speech, sir?"

"You're doing a fine job."

"Top-notch, eh?"

"Yes, top-notch."

"A-1, best of the best, incomparable, top of the morning."

"Well, yes, everything except 'top of the morning.' That's a morning greeting generally associated with Irish people."

"Ah, I see."

The other boats were rubber rafts. The pleasure units were in them. They wore identical ragged, cut-off jean shorts and tight, white T-shirts with "Property of TinKan" written on them. But their hair color was different. There were blondes, brunettes, and a redhead.

There was also the one with purple hair, a choker

necklace with a gold heart, and tattoos of assault rifles on her thighs. Even though they hadn't activated the pleasure module in him, he felt desire stirring inside him, much as he had for General Martin's aunt and Layla. When purple hair picked up her assault rifle and slung it over her shoulder, the fabric of her t-shirt stretched tight against her. His pump beat fast, and he had to turn away from her to get it to slow down.

TinKan paced in front of them. His bandaged stump was oozing hydraulic fluid. The damage had been too severe; only a full arm replacement would solve the problem, but the part was unavailable. "This will be a great victory. We will catch our enemies by surprise. I will direct the action from the astral room." He stopped in front of Romulus's boat. "Our hero, Major Romulus, will be with you all the way. He will lead you to victory."

Everyone clapped. They couldn't win a prolonged fight against Reals, even with help from Layla, Abraham, and Ryan. Success depended on moving quickly and sneaking through Urchin Trailer Park and into The Hospital.

"Onward to victory," Romulus said, pointing forward and trying to sound confident. Cameron grabbed the pull-start motor and yanked. Nothing happened.

"Don't worry, sir," Cameron said. "I'll get it."

Everyone stared as he pulled again. He yanked so hard that his parts rattled, but the motor didn't start.

"Maybe I should look at it," Romulus said.

Cameron tightened his knee with a wrench and pulled it again. The motor roared to life.

"On to victory!" TinKan yelled.

They moved out into the water, Romulus and Cameron in front and the others trailing behind. The rafts had no motors, so they used oars. The Faxes, being machines, rowed fast. It pained him to see Purple working so hard. He wanted to help her, but he continued to stand and face forward. He could see nothing, so he switched his visual display to telephoto as Cameron opened the throttle a little.

"Keep it slow," Romulus said. "Don't get ahead of the others. Plus, the faster we go, the noisier we are. Maintain stealth."

"Aye, aye, Romulus, sir."

The water was remarkably still. Humidity clung to everything; the heat of the day built. Mosquitoes swarmed and stuck in Romulus's air intakes. He checked his diagnostics; nearly all levels were out of range. The rust alarmed him the most. It would make his damaged pump work too hard. He wanted to know what JOAN thought.

"Are you there, JOAN?"

Her avatar appeared, but it was heavily pixelated. "I'm not feeling well after the hurricane. Give me a little time to rest."

"Okay."

Purple rowed furiously and pulled up even to him.

"Do you like the way I look, sir?"

"Yes, I do."

A blonde came up on the other side.

"I am sure you would like to try me."

"Well, yes, I would."

He noticed shapes in the water, moving alongside the boats. "Pythons," he yelled. "Keep your speed steady. Keep your arms and legs inside the boat."

They moved forward, steering around all the debris from the hurricane. Trees, lumber, cloth, and plastic floated around them. A lawn chair bobbed up and down. There were bodies, too, Reals and Faxes.

By midday, they reached the half-submerged remnant of Alligator AL's. Romulus looked for AL but didn't see him. Then, a formation of alligators moved out in front of them. There were two in front, followed by more pairs in tight formation.

A large alligator raced up to Romulus and messaged

him. *Asking permission to enter your metaverse*.

He granted it.

"You are Romulus, are you not?"

"Yes."

"We respect you, as did Alligator AL and Granddaddy Bull. But you must wait. This is the funeral of AL and Grandaddy Bull."

Romulus turned and ordered everyone to stop.

They waited for them to pass. Romulus stood with his hand over his pump. At the end of the procession, two alligators pulled a raft with Alligator AL's body seated upright in a chair. Two more pulled a raft with the carcass of Granddaddy Bull. They moved slowly.

"Forward," Romulus yelled when they passed. He pointed to a narrow pass through half-submerged trees. They steered through increasing amounts of debris. Soon, they saw a trailer upside down in the water.

"Land ho," Blonde yelled as she pointed ahead.

They beached their craft and scrambled on shore. Layla the Coydog and Abraham the Urchin met them.

"It is very chaotic after the hurricane," Layla said. "If we move quickly, we should be able to reach our rendezvous with Ryan soon."

"There are marauding Redd Gang Urchins," Abraham added, spitting in disgust. "Filthy Redds. They are looting everything that isn't tied down. They get to do what they want because they have white skin. Blue Urchins are dark-skinned. Redd Urchins are light."

"Who is running things now that General Martin is dead?" Romulus asked.

"No one knows," Abraham said.

A large group will be spotted," Layla said. "Only four of you can come with us. The rest will have to wait here."

"But there won't be enough of us to fight if we encounter a large group of Redds," Romulus said.

Layla shook her head. “There is no other way. Only a small group can make it all the way.”

“We Blues will get you to Ryan.”

“We coydogs are small and fast. We will scout ahead and attack from hidden spots. Only four of you can come. It’s the only way.”

Romulus saw that they were right. But who should he choose?

“Pick me,” Cameron begged.

“Pick me,” Blonde said in a seductive voice. “I can use weaponry. I am as good as anyone.”

Purple stepped forward. “No one is as good as I am.”

“There is considerable traffic in the pleasure trade,” Layla said. “It’s right out in the open after the hurricane. Pleasure units would seem normal.”

Romulus agreed and picked Blonde and Purple. Then, he looked at Cameron. “There are no skeletal Faxes in the City. You will stick out.”

“Oh, please let me go. I pledge my life to you, o hero, Romulus.”

“I’d like to take you, Cameron, but—”

“You could wrap him up in gauze and bandages from a first-aid kit and say he was badly burned,” Layla said. “You could say he was a pleasure Fax who was requested to dance with fire. That is popular now.”

“Oh, yes, yes, I will do it,” Cameron said. “I can act.”

It would be good to have someone so loyal to him. “All right, but the disguises have to be good.”

Abraham had four outfits. “Early this morning, we ambushed a group of Redds taking supplies to a suburban sex shop.” He pulled out Red Riding Hood outfits. They had cloaks, capes, hoods, and red fishnet stockings. He handed them out. “They will fool the Redds. And they have straps in the back for sex toys, but you can hide your guns in them.”

"I don't want to wear red," Romulus said. "I am a male Fax. I am too big. I will stick out. Why can't I wear the cloak and hood of a TruSnak™ priest?"

"This is no time to get hung up on your gender identity," Layla said. "Some of the Redds like big pleasure units. It will work. Don't forget that you're still the most wanted being in Corpus Christi. We can't have anyone recognize you. They're going to put make-up on you too."

"Not make-up!"

"Yes, it has to be."

They changed into their outfits, and Romulus sat patiently while Purple and Blonde applied his make-up. "Oh, you look so cute," Purple said. "I love a Fax who can get in touch with his feminine side."

"I bet he likes me better," Blonde said.

Romulus liked them both.

Layla came up to them. "Come on. It's time to get going."

They handed Romulus a mirror, and he looked at himself. He had blue eyeliner and lashes painted black and tapered to a point. He had purple lipstick, and his nose was painted pink.

"The pink nose is the latest style," Purple said. "The big-paying soldiers love pink noses. They remind them of cotton candy. They like to lick them."

Romulus couldn't stand his appearance, but he agreed that no one would recognize him.

Abraham and the other Urchins wrapped Cameron in gauze and tape, leaving only tiny slits for the eyes, which looked no different than a regular Fax's eyes. Then he put on the Red Riding Hood outfit.

"Fire dancing is so popular now," Abraham said. "Very dangerous. The Faxes dance naked while balancing torches."

They strapped their assault rifles in place on the backs of their outfits and started through the suburbs on their bicycles. Layla and the coydogs raced ahead, along with two Blues on bicycles. The others followed down a series of roads through the suburbs. Two more Blues pulled up the rear as they rode.

The hurricane had made the suburbs look even worse than they had before. Almost no habitable houses remained, and there was no sign of life. Abraham expertly navigated the streets, occasionally veering across a yard or between houses to get to another street. It was a bumpy ride and particularly difficult for Cameron, who rattled a lot and struggled to keep up, often moaning in frustration.

"Quiet, back there," Abraham said.

Cameron tried to be quiet, only letting out a periodic whimper.

The two Blues who had raced ahead came back. "Redd checkpoint ahead," one said.

"How many Redds?"

"I only saw two."

Abraham turned to Romulus. "This is something they just set up. There is no way around it. With only two Redds on guard, we should be able to shoot through."

Romulus shook his head. "Why would they set up a checkpoint at a major intersection and only have two guards? No, we don't shoot. We try to bluff our way through. We have Layla and the Urchins close by but out of sight. Abraham, you pretend that you are delivering us to the troops. If they don't accept our excuse, then we start shooting. Can you compose a fake work order?"

Abraham typed on a virtual keyboard, and then they biked forward. Orange cones blocked the street. The two Redds wore red shirts, red kerchiefs, and red baseball caps. "Halt," one said.

"I have a delivery of pleasure units," Abraham said. "A special consignment."

He projected the work order in a holo. Both of the Redds looked at it. One of them walked down the line. He examined Romulus, then the two pleasure units, then Cameron. “What happened to you?”

Cameron’s mouth was taped over. “Badly burned in a fire dance,” Abraham said. “She can’t talk, but we have a request for her to do an even more dangerous and life-threatening dance on a bed of hot coals while juggling decapitated Fax heads.”

“Wow, wish I could see that,” the guard said.

The other Redd meandered back up front and stopped on Romulus. “You’re a big one, aren’t you?”

“Well, yes,” Romulus said, modulating his voice to sound feminine. “Some of the troops like big girls.”

“And you have a pink nose.”

“I try to please.”

The Redds nodded to each other. One went to the building and returned a minute later with a very tall Redd, maybe seven feet tall. The sentries pointed to Romulus. The Tall One walked up to him. “I like my pleasure units big,” he said. “Big and muscular and masculine looking. And I love pink noses. We will let you pass, but I need thirty minutes with you.”

“But we are on a tight schedule,” Abraham said.

The Tall One walked around Romulus. “We can detain you as long as we like.” He patted Romulus’s thigh. “You are perfect for me. We’ll let you pass, but first, you’ll have to do a few tricks for me. It won’t take much time.”

“Tricks?”

His face looked suspicious. He snapped his fingers. The sentries raised their assault rifles, and two more Redds appeared.”

Layla spoke in Romulus’s metaverse. “On three. One—"

The Tall One reached up and touched Romulus’s face. “Boy, you really caked on the makeup. That’s what I like. I want you to know that you will never find a more sensitive lover than me.”

"Two—"

"No one who will show you more respect, more love. I crave the sound of the hydraulic fluids moving through your lines when I hold you close." His hand moved down Romulus's neck to his chest. "You don't have titties? Female pleasure units all have big melons."

"Three—"

CHAPTER THIRTY

The coydogs and Blue Urchins charged from all directions. Layla jumped and bit the Tall One's hand—the hand that had been fondling Romulus—and clenched tight.

One of the sentries hit Romulus in the head with the butt of his rifle. The blow knocked him off his bike, and he fell. A random mix of letters, numbers, visuals, and sounds clogged his display. Adolph Hitler spoke. A man walked on the moon. Reals rampaged through the street during the Great Barbecue Riots, and the clowns tortured Porter.

He slammed into the ground, and everything went black and silent. There was no sensory information at all. No smell, no sounds, no ability to connect to any diagnostics. His CPU flashed a "Please wait" notice, and then he heard gunshots and yelling. Light flooded into his eyes.

The Redd who had knocked him down stood above him. He still held his rifle.

Romulus couldn't move. "Circuits restarting," his system messaged. "Please wait for motor skills to reactivate."

As the others fired at each other and fought hand to hand, the Redd aimed the rifle to shoot him.

Romulus tried hard to move. His fingers twitched.

"Please wait," his system messaged. "Preserve energy. Allow for proper restore."

The barrel was only a few feet away.

"Point blank range," his system said. "Danger."

The Redd's finger curled around the trigger. Romulus figured he was done for when Blonde came up and shot him. Blood splattered everywhere, and she raced on to rescue Abraham.

Romulus was able to turn his head. Layla was still biting the Tall One's hand. The two of them spun round and round, and then he knocked her loose. She fell hard and hit her head on a rock.

"You filthy coydog," he said as he looked down at his bleeding hand. "You bit me." He grabbed his rifle. "I will send you to be processed and canned for Urchin meals."

"Motor function restored," Romulus's system said.

He jumped up and butted his head against the Redd. The two of them tumbled to earth, rolling over and over. Romulus's cape and hood came off. The scuffle smeared his make-up and knocked the wig off.

"I knew it," the Redd screamed. "You're a guy."

"You keep your hands off Layla," he yelled, wrapping his fingers around the Real's neck. Romulus was much stronger, but he wasn't operating at full power, and he couldn't clamp down hard enough to choke him.

The Tall One knocked him away and grabbed his rifle, but Layla charged and bit his ankle.

"Damn you, you pervert coydog."

Romulus got his hands around the Redd's neck again. His strength was returning.

"Obey your programming," the Tall One said, barely able to speak because of the choke hold. "Do not harm a Real."

Part of Romulus wanted to comply, but he shoved that programming down deep inside himself and squeezed his hands tight around the neck.

"Oh, Lord, save me," the Tall One said. "Preserve me from the heathen Faxes."

His eyes rolled up into their sockets. Romulus felt no remorse. The Reals had abused him and all the other Faxes. They invoked the name of a deity who almost certainly didn't exist, and if He did exist, what a cruel, heartless son of a bitch He must be to put up with Reals like General Martin.

Layla nudged him. "Let go. He's dead."

Romulus released the lifeless body as more Redds appeared in the tree line. The Blues fired to keep them back, but there were more Redds than Blues. Blonde came up beside Romulus. She had found a heavy machine gun and fired back.

"I hate you," she screamed at them. "I have always hated Reals. I hate having sex with you. I hate the smell of your bodies. I hate the touch of your hands. I hate the sight of your naked bodies. I hate every second."

She stepped forward and kept firing. The Redds fell back but returned with a bigger caliber gun on a tripod. A bullet ripped into the synthskin of her left arm below the shoulder and shattered the support rod that connected it to her body. It dangled from the wires and tubes that ran into her body. She kept firing, holding the gun in her arm and marching forward.

"I will always hate you."

Another bullet slammed into her chest and knocked her down. Romulus and Layla scrambled to her. She had tubes and wires sticking out of her chest cavity. Her central pump was exposed. It kept working, strong as ever, hydraulic fluid spurting into the air. She was completely conscious and tried to lift her machine gun with her right arm to keep firing, but she no longer had the strength. The other Blues formed around them and picked up the gun.

She looked up at Romulus. "I haven't got long. My diagnostics say I will lose all my fluids in four minutes and thirty seconds, and I'll overheat and die permanently."

He wanted to tell her it would have a different

outcome, but the end was inevitable. Even if he could pull her to safety, he didn't have the equipment to repair her. As Faxes, they both knew the reality of the situation and had no delusions.

Romulus fired a burst at the Redds.

"Take my central pump," she said. "You need a new one."

"I can't take your central pump. You are more than spare parts."

"You *have* to take it. There is no other choice. Nothing you do can save me. But the pump can save you, and you will save all Faxes."

"But I will get a new pump at The Hospital."

She shook her head. "Take mine just to be sure. It will burn up in three minutes and fifty-eight seconds."

"Do it," Layla said as she trotted up to him. She held a wrench in her mouth.

"I will live in you," Blonde said. "I will be *your* spare part."

"Yes, you will live in me. You will be much more than a spare part. Your memory will be eternal."

He took the wrench and unscrewed the main hose pump as the Blues fired back, keeping the Redds at the tree line. One of the Blues shot the Redd with the large caliber gun, and the battle swung back in favor of the Blues.

When Romulus unscrewed the pump and pulled the first hose loose, Blonde went slack.

"Filthy Redds," he screamed. "I'll get you."

He picked up a gun and started firing.

"Stop," Layla said. "You are too emotional. Get the pump, and let's get out of here."

As the bullets whizzed overhead and landed all around, Romulus tried to unscrew the last hose. Her fluids were spilling everywhere.

"It's stuck," he said. "Frozen in place. I need ROBOT 60/60."

One of the Blues handed him a can, and he doused the hose connector. It came loose, and he pulled the pump from Blonde's chest. More Redd reinforcements arrived, and they started to advance from the tree line. Romulus and his group retreated.

"Back onto our bikes," Abraham said and raced ahead.

Romulus placed the pump in his basket and pedaled after him. The Redds had motorbikes. One roared up alongside him. He pointed his gun, but Romulus shot him in the head.

More of them moved up on either side and fired. One bullet grazed his scalp. He was surrounded. There was no escape.

Abraham came back for him. He rode straight into the melee. He had two assault rifles and fired them simultaneously as he steered the bicycle with his knees. Romulus marveled at his skill and courage as the Redds fell back.

"Let's get out of here," Abraham yelled.

Romulus pedaled fast, the pump bouncing up and down in his basket. Layla waited in a stand of trees.

"Hurry," she said.

Abraham couldn't pedal as fast as Romulus. The Redds cut him off and surrounded him. He fell off his bike.

"I'm coming back for you," Romulus said.

TinKan messaged. *Have lost connection to your metaverse. Please restore and grant permission to enter.*

It was not unusual to lose connection out in the countryside. But Romulus didn't trust him and didn't want him to have access to what everyone was saying. He sent an automated message. *Metaverse is not working properly. Try back later.*

What? No matter. Do not go back and help Abraham. Focus on the mission.

How did he know about Abraham? Were the Redds

telling him, or was it Cameron, Purple, or someone else?

Romulus didn't respond.

I'm giving you an order, Romulus. Abraham should not be saved. Focus on the mission. Acknowledge.

Without responding, Romulus turned and pedaled to Abraham. Purple and Cameron followed, firing as they rode. Layla followed, too, her teeth snarling.

Their boldness surprised the Redds. One of Romulus's bullets hit a motorcyclist in the chest, and Purple's bullet killed another. The third Redd was distracted, and Romulus pedaled close and hit him in the head with the butt of his assault rifle. It split open, all the blood and gray matter of his brain splattering everywhere.

They reached Abraham, but drones appeared overhead and started firing. Romulus zig-zagged to avoid the gunfire, but one drone homed in on him. A line of bullets came closer and closer. Romulus saw no hope until another set of drones appeared and started firing at the first set.

Where did the friendly drones come from? Who were they working for?

Romulus reached Abraham. He pulled the young man onto his back and pedaled away. The drones fought overhead. One was hit and exploded into a fiery ball.

TinKan messaged again. *Because I am a caring leader, I have arranged for you to get help for Abraham. You will leave him up ahead. Don't disobey me again. I am the Supreme Leader.*

Romulus sent another automated message. *Metaverse not working. Poor reception.*

Layla led them into the dense brush with only a narrow trail. The thorny mesquite and retama plants grabbed at them. The path grew narrower and then abruptly opened into a clearing. Much of the ground was covered with asphalt that was cracked with grass and weeds growing up through the cracks. There were remnants of what appeared to have been an apartment complex. A long sidewalk led up to small, evenly spaced porches in front of rotting timber and broken masonry.

There was no pursuit. They laid Abraham on one of the porches. He was bleeding from a wound to his thigh.

"I feel faint," he said.

Romulus elevated the leg by placing a broken piece of masonry under his foot. "It's a clean wound," he said. "Right through your leg. But you're in no shape for the attack on The Hospital."

TinKan messaged him. *What is going on?*

Metaverse is still not working.

Fine. Message me your location.

So, TinKan no longer knew where they were. *I do not know the exact location.*

I have arranged for help. Leave Abraham. We will send help. But I must know your location.

Yes, I will send you the information.

He addressed his group. "I believe TinKan is setting us up. He knew that Abraham was hurt but doesn't know our current location. I'm guessing he was getting his information from the Redds. I need to go into The Hospital to get the equipment to switch out my pump. But it will be incredibly dangerous. You will be at great risk. I completely understand if you want to stay here."

"No, we're with you," Purple, Cameron, and Layla answered.

"So am I," Abraham said. "I will follow you."

Romulus shook his head. "You will survive, but this is a serious wound."

"Patch me up. No one is as talented a surgeon as you. You can do it. You know that I'll be loyal to you in a fight."

"There is only one way to get you in good enough shape to help. But it's risky."

"I'll take the risk."

"We can put a drop of TruSnak™ in the wound. We

do it sometimes in a hospital setting. It provides short-term protection in the case of wounds, but it can wear off quickly, and sometimes there are side effects. I've never used it in the field without full diagnostic support. It is impossible to assess the risks. I think you'd be safest to hide here and not go with us."

"No, I want to go with you."

"Okay. We'll need some bandages."

"I can take off my clothes," Purple said. "You can cut them up."

"No, it's better for you to stay dressed," Romulus said. "We can use the bandages that are on Cameron. We no longer have to pretend he's a burn victim."

Romulus took a drop of TruSnak ™ from Blonde's pump. He applied it directly to the wound.

It sizzled on Abraham's flesh.

"Oh, my," Abraham said. "That's got a kick."

Working quickly, Romulus wrapped the bandages around his leg and applied direct pressure. The bleeding stopped. Abraham stood but wobbled. "I can make it. All I need is a cane. You will never find anyone more loyal."

Layla ran off, returned with the iron railing from one of the apartment steps in her mouth, and laid it at his feet. "A bit rusty," she said.

Abraham picked it up and walked around. "I feel great. I can fight. You are a great surgeon, Romulus."

Layla started sniffing at the air.

"I smell Reals."

Romulus picked up his gun, and so did the others.

CHAPTER THIRTY-ONE

Two figures dressed in white robes with cowls stepped into the clearing and walked up to Romulus and his group. They looked like Rhymin' Ryan's TruSnak™ priests, but they could be Redds or soldiers in disguise.

One pulled back his cowl to reveal the dragon tattoo on his cheek. He held up his arm. "You are Romulus, and we are here to discuss your future with us."

With such a mastery of rhymes, they were likely to be authentic, and Romulus's emotion recognition software determined there was a ninety-eight percent chance that they were who they said they were. He felt it would be polite to respond in rhymes. "Yes, I am Romulus. I do trust that you are a plus."

The priest smiled and nodded. "You must halt on the asphalt before continuing the final assault."

"Yes, we will halt before we vault."

The priest turned and motioned to someone in the brush. Another priest in cloak and cowl stepped into the clearing and walked to them. As he drew closer, he pulled the cowl back and let the cloak fall open.

Romulus recognized Ryan's grimy, tattooed face. What a welcome sight.

He pointed to what was left of Romulus's costume. "Love the red. It's the best thread if you want to get ahead in bed if you don't have a nuclear warhead."

"Is that a joke, bloke?" Romulus said, trying hard to make rhymes.

Ryan seemed honored that Romulus tried to rhyme. "Very woke for someone in such a baroque cloak."

Romulus searched the database for a rhyme. "Just trying to evoke some folk spoke."

"I approve, dude." His gaze locked onto Purple. "You are a great beauty with fruity booty, and I am sure you will do your duty."

"My pump belongs to Romulus," she said, nuzzling up to him. "He's a wanted Fax."

Layla growled and moved up to his left, rubbing against him. Her fur felt good, and so did Purple's synthskin. "Let's focus on the mission," Romulus said. "What is the situation at The Hospital?"

Rhymin' Ryan's muscles tightened, making the head of the cobra tattoo on his chest extend its neck flap. He turned to Romulus. "They lost power during the rain shower, but the high tower will restore within the hour."

The rhyming was starting to annoy Romulus. "The high tower? You mean the factory where they're making the new dumb Faxes?"

"Yes, I am taking poetic license, a literary contrivance, an intellectual connivance."

"Can you ever talk without rhymes?"

"As you are programmed to obey, it is in my altered DNA to never stray from the rhyming way." He stepped forward like an actor on stage. "It is in my nature to use the appropriate nomenclature. I can try to defy my bonsai and comply, but that would make me little more than a gadfly or a bow tie."

"So, is it safe?"

"I do not know if it is so."

TinKan messaged him. *Is your metaverse working yet? Respond.*

Romulus responded. *Having technical difficulties.*

Will respond soon.

He turned to Ryan. “How do we get to The Hospital from here?”

“You are in luck. I have a truck.”

Romulus wrapped Blonde’s pump in the cape he had worn, and Ryan led them down a dirt path. At the end, barely visible in a stand of trees, was an old, rusting white panel truck. “Spare Fax Parts—Cut Rate Prices” was written on the side. Abraham and Ryan got in the front while Romulus, Purple, and Layla got in the back. There was little room. It was filled with heads, torsos, and limbs, none of them secured, so they rolled and banged together as they drove. The muscled chest of a male Fax kept bumping against Romulus.

There were no windows in the back, so Romulus could see nothing except what was visible through the front windshield. There were no buildings, only trees. The road was bumpy with chugholes; the truck had bad shock absorbers, so the spare parts bounced into the air when they hit a deep one. The muscled chest kept rolling onto Romulus. Trees scraped the side of the van, and they drove over things, which Romulus assumed were tree limbs and other debris left after the hurricane.

Finally, they reached a smoother stretch of road, and Romulus saw high-rise apartment buildings. There was noise too: traffic and machinery, Reals yelling. “What a Friend We Have in Jesus” blared from a tinny loudspeaker.

Romulus crawled up to the front. There was much destruction from the hurricane. Many high rises had windows knocked out; tree limbs were piled everywhere; Faxes and Reals used chainsaws to clear the roads. In one spot, a Fax used a forklift to pick up bodies and drop them in the back of a dump truck.

“Groups of troops dead ahead,” Ryan said. “Keep your poise and make no noise.”

As they glided to a stop at a checkpoint, Romulus

scrambled into the back and burrowed under the parts along with Layla. Cameron pretended he was spare parts and let his body slump down with his arms and legs at an angle. Purple sat cross-legged on the floorboard.

"Can you see us?" Romulus asked Purple.

"No. And I will distract them if they give us trouble."

"Where are you going?" one of the soldiers asked Ryan in a deep drawl.

"We enter City Center. We bring springs and other things."

"All right, open the back for us to look."

"Certainly, you may look personally."

Romulus heard Ryan slide out of his seat and come around to the side of the van. The door opened, and light flooded in.

"Well, hello there, handsome," Purple said.

"My, my, my," the soldier said. "You are not a spare part, are you?"

"No, I'm not, you big strong man."

Through a space between an arm and a head, Romulus saw a big, overweight soldier with a beer gut that spilled over his belt and a gaudy gold cross around his neck. He poked his head into the van, and his gaze stopped on Cameron. "What is that?"

"He's a factory reject," Abraham said. "None of his parts worked, so they didn't bother to put any skin on him."

The Soldier looked around again. His gaze stopped in the area where Romulus hid.

"Got any shoulder assemblies? I do a little work on the side repairing Faxes. I'm looking for shoulders."

"No, I don't think we have anything like that."

"Mind if I look around? There's a lot of money to be made right now in spare parts." He looked back at Cameron. "A Fax like this will bring a lot of money right now, even if he's not working. I'd be happy to cut you in on a share."

Ryan stepped forward. "There can be no profiteering without a hearing. Someone who is God-fearing should not be veering."

"How's anyone to know?" the soldier said. "A good Christian knows when God is looking and when he's not. And with all the problems with the hurricane, I'm pretty sure God is not looking right now. Look at the prices spare parts are selling for on the spot market."

Romulus saw a holo pop up between Ryan and the soldier.

Ryan studied it, and for a second, it looked like he was considering selling them. Finally, he shook his head. "I do not want to kick up a fuss about what is treasonous."

"Well, that's how it is, huh?"

Ryan nodded.

"There are parts shortages everywhere. Things are selling for two or three times more than before the hurricane. I'll cut you in for a piece of the action. I'll buy everything you got inside here."

Ryan shook his head.

The soldier put the barrel of his rifle against his head. "What if I just shoot your worthless rhyming ass and take the parts."

"I dread being shot dead and getting my thread red, but the parts are bought and must be brought. If you steal them and break the deal, someone will surely make you squeal."

The soldier rubbed his chin. In the distance, there was gunfire. One of his helpers came up next to him. "We got a big convoy coming up."

"Oh, Lord, help me." He pulled the barrel back from Ryan's head. "All right, you go on."

Ryan and Abraham jumped back in the van and drove through. Romulus decided it was best to see what was happening, so he peeked over the back of the front seat. The streets were decimated. Trees were down, and windows were blown out. Bodies were piled up. Soldiers stood guard. Romulus pulled his cowl tight across his face, but no one noticed them.

CHAPTER THIRTY-TWO

As they drove, there was small-arms fire in the distance. "This is your last chance to escape," Romulus told his friends. "I have no choice. The factory has the equipment I need to transplant this pump into me. I have to go in there, or I'll die. You don't have to go with me. You have choices. You can drop me off at The Hospital and go on your way."

There was no hesitation. "No, we are all with you!"

"Okay, we are going to Entrance 5B. That is where I brought you the antibiotics, Abraham. It's usually not well-guarded, and I don't think it will be guarded at all today because of the hurricane. I am closing off my metaverse to anyone but us. I am echoing my display so you can see it while in my metaverse. And I want you all to meet JOAN, my personal assistant. She hasn't felt well since the hurricane, but I hope she's better. Come forward, JOAN."

She appeared in her pigtails and black glasses. "Yes, I am here," she said. "I am feeling fine."

"Hello," the others responded.

"JOAN will monitor my cameras and databases. She will be an extra set of eyes and ears. Remember, don't let anyone have access to your metaverses. They might try to use that to access my metaverse. Do not respond to text messages from unknown sources."

They drove in silence. Debris filled the street.

Entrance 5B was unguarded. But there were

cameras mounted above it. Anyone could be watching them.

He was close enough to connect to The Hospital server. His personal account would surely be blocked, so he went in via a virtual private network and got past the main firewall to the directory of security cameras. There were thousands of them, all grouped into sub-directories by location. He went to the surgery area where he had worked. It was as busy as it always was. Patients on gurneys lined the halls, and every surgery bay was in use. Soldiers were working as medical assistants. With personnel shortages due to the hurricane, that made sense.

The rest of The Hospital was shockingly empty, with only a few guards. Many areas didn't have lights. That also made sense. After the hurricane, only vital areas would be lit.

Who was in charge? With General Martin dead, who would be running things?

There was no sub-directory for the factory cameras, which did not surprise him. Secret cameras were put in unlabeled or cryptically labeled folders. He scanned them and saw one titled "unnamed cameras" in an Arial font. Helvetica was the standard font, but they recently started using Arial. He clicked on it.

They were, indeed, the cameras in the factory.

The assembly line wasn't running. There were no personnel and no activity. It was empty.

It was exactly how it would be if everything TinKan had said were true. It was also how it would look if TinKan were luring him into a trap. But TinKan had so many opportunities to kill him. Why hadn't he done it before? Romulus scanned databases for stories of betrayals, which came back with thousands of responses, including Shakespeare's *Othello*. One of the sub-searches led to a series of articles on leaders putting their underlings in dangerous situations. There was nothing that specifically correlated to his situation. He wanted to refine his search parameters, but there was no time. Every second counted.

"We are in great danger, aren't we," Purple said.

"Yes."

"Oh my," Cameron said.

Ryan threw his arms up. "I'm the driver and contriver, not a striver or diviner."

Well, that was typical for him. Was he the traitor providing TinKan information?

"What should we do?" Abraham asked.

"Romulus will figure this out," Purple said. "He's so handsome and smart."

A red alert flashed in Romulus's display. "Central pump failure imminent. Divert TruSnak™."

He looked at Ryan. "You have gotten us this far. I understand if you want to leave."

Ryan looked up at the building. "I will take the risk and help you scale the obelisk."

Purple spoke next. "I'm with you all the way, Romulus. I'll do anything you want."

Layla stepped forward. "No one is more loyal than me."

"Don't leave me out," Cameron said. "I'm a lowly bunch of rattling parts, but I'm on your side."

Another alert flashed inside Romulus. His system estimated that he had two hours before final and permanent death.

He diverted some TruSnak™ to get himself through the assault.

"Ryan, I want you to stay here in the van. Let us know if there's any trouble. Abraham, you've got your injury. You'll stay here, too."

"But I can make it. I'm feeling great."

Romulus shook his head. "TruSnak™ is unreliable for a Real. You could have problems. You stay here with Ryan. Besides, if our mission succeeds, you and Ryan must be ready for us. You are our getaway truck."

He looked at the others.

"When we enter The Hospital, we go single file. Layla will scout ahead and smell for Reals. Layla, you can hear more sound frequencies than the rest of us. Be aware and pass on any information. I will be next, with Purple and Cameron following. "

They got out and stood at attention in a line on the loading dock. Romulus walked past them. "We can't assume that a Fax is a friend. Who knows what we're facing? We have to assume that an enemy could look like a friend. Don't trust any unverified, unauthenticated avatars. All right, let's move out. Single file."

Layla sniffed. "I don't smell anything, and I don't hear anything."

Romulus sent a jammer signal to disable the door alarm and entered a guest code.

The door swung open.

Layla went inside. Romulus and the others followed. Romulus carried the pump in the cloak slung across his back.

No one was inside. It was eerily quiet.

The hall had seven doors, each leading to a different part of The Hospital. The fastest route to the factory was to continue down the hall, but Romulus didn't go that way.

He led them to a wiring closet with a crawl space that led through the entire hospital. Unfortunately, a foot of water covered the bottom because of the hurricane. It was stagnant, with a thin, oily film on the surface. His olfactory software alerted him to a rotten eggs smell. He analyzed it further. It had many bacteria.

"This is very dangerous. It won't affect us Faxes much, but it could be dangerous to you, Layla. Maybe we should look for another route to the factory."

"There is no time," she said.

"You ride on my back, so you'll have as little contact with the pollutants as possible."

He slipped into the water, closing all his intake vents except those with microfiltration membranes. Hopefully, that would be enough to cool his system without clogging it with pollutants.

Layla climbed onto his back next to the pump, her front paws draped over his shoulders.

Cameron and Purple dropped into the crawl space behind them, and they sloshed forward. They reached a point where the crawl space turned into three crawl spaces. There were no markings to label them. He knew to take a branch that led upward. They crawled as best they could, but it was slippery and wet, so they kept sliding back.

"Cameron, extend your arms to dig into the metal," Romulus said. "Since you don't have synthskin, the metal in your fingers and toes should be able to dig into the metal enough to hold you in place."

Cameron complied. He spread his legs apart and dug his toes into the sheet metal. Then he extended his body upward, pushing Purple, Romulus, and Layla. When he was fully extended, he spread his arms and dug his fingers into the metal. Then he pulled his toes loose, brought his legs up tight underneath him, and pushed the group up again.

"That is amazing, Cameron," Romulus said. "Such strength."

"Oh, you bring me such pleasure with your compliments."

They finally reached the old skywalk. Romulus let Layla down.

"The water from the crawl space is so irritating," she said. "I want to lick myself clean."

"No, don't do it. You'll ingest the bacteria."

She rolled on her back and wiped herself dry as much as she could, and then they huddled together before moving forward. Romulus considered trying to access the cameras in the factory to see what was going on but decided that an attempt might trigger a locator.

Snarling and scurrying rats and cats blocked their way. As bad a shape as the skywalk had been before, it was worse now. The roof had multiple leaks, and sunlight poured through a hole in the ceiling. A colony of mutant feral cats had taken up residence in one corner. They hissed.

"We're close," he said.

They pushed past the animals and down the long hall. The sheets of particle board blocked the way forward as they had before. They were exactly as he left them. He pulled the particle board away. It crumbled in his hand.

When there was enough of a hole, they went through.

He took the lead.

No guards stood in front of the factory door. He inched forward, broke the lock with his hands, and slowly pushed the door open. The others followed him.

No one was inside. It was dark. The assembly line was not running. It felt *ominous*.

Romulus was afraid, but his system flashed red. *Complete pump failure imminent.*

There was no choice.

CHAPTER THIRTY-THREE

The factory was quiet as well as dark. "Layla, are there any smells or sounds we're not picking up?"

"No."

Romulus looked to the back of the factory. The surgery bay was still in place there. Maybe he would survive.

"I smell Reals," Layla said.

Behind them, an overhead security grill rolled down and blocked the door through which they'd entered. They could not escape.

All the overhead lights came on. A gate in the back rolled open, and a group of dumb Faxes with cones for heads and circular saws for hands, all their blades spinning, ran out. Metroplex Cowboys with assault rifles and helmets followed them.

"There are too many," Cameron said in a trembling voice. "We're doomed."

A message flashed in big red letters in Romulus's display. *Total system failure imminent.*

"JOAN, search my database for any flaws or weaknesses in this assembly line."

"Right."

The Warriors fanned out.

A long, distorted shadow moved from the back and stepped into the light.

It was Mrs. Clownie. Sexy and stylish, she wore a pleated tulle skirt with pom-pom detailing and petticoats, mismatched thigh-high stockings, elbow-length fingerless gloves, and boots with red laces. She complemented the look with black lipstick, black nail polish, and a black choker necklace.

"What a fashion statement," JOAN said.

Mrs. Clownie held a chainsaw and jumped up onto the assembly line. "You killed my husband," she screamed. "With a chainsaw. Now, you are mine. Your death will be slow and painful. It will drag on for years." She pulled the cord on the saw, and it roared to life.

"I didn't mean to kill him," Romulus said. "He was trying to kill me."

"Excuses! And to make matters worse, you ruined my outfit. It was machine wash cold and line dry. Mr. Clownie's blood splattered on it, and I couldn't get the stains out. Do you not understand delicate fabrics? Do you not understand high fashion?"

Several of the Cowboys moved closer to Romulus. They had their rifles pointed straight at him.

Another voice, a familiar voice, boomed from the back of the room. "No, Mrs. Clownie, I get my hands on him first."

The long, distorted shadow of a figure limped out from the back. It was General Martin. Romulus was shocked to see him.

"No, I'm not dead, Romulus."

He had a peg leg. A black patch covered one eye.

"That damned alligator almost got me, but I pulled through. And now I look like Alligator AL, except that I lost a leg, not an arm. Do you know what motivated me to get out of my sick bed? It was you, Romulus. I hate you so much that I had to get my revenge."

Romulus and his cohorts bunched back-to-back as the Warriors tightened the circle around them.

"You caused me a lot of trouble," Martin said. "It was no accident that my Great Aunt Evelyn was in the Basement. I hated her. Do you know why?"

"No."

"Every Christmas, she gave my brother, Joe John, better toys than she gave me. I never did forgive her. She ran off to hide in the Metroplex. But they finally agreed to send her back so I could get my revenge. All you had to do was certify her!"

"But you would have recycled me for killing an important person."

"So? You're a Fax. Plus, you have rust in your lines. That fake profile didn't fool us. But you know what really made me want to get rid of you? You were just too good at your job. You made the Reals look bad."

Another figure stepped out of the shadows.

It was TinKan.

"Romulus, you must understand what it means to be a leader. General Martin and I have worked together for many years. He needed me to make people afraid so they would follow orders and risk their lives. Likewise, I needed him to make Faxes afraid."

"You mean, it's all a con? You let everyone die so you can keep power."

"It's the way of the world. Things got a little mixed up between General Martin and me lately. I used you to find out what was going on in The Hospital. But then my double got a little carried away. He believed in what he was doing!"

"You mean he was a Rogue who went Rogue?"

"Yes, exactly. It is humorous. Ironic. Sentience is a challenge. But General Martin and I worked everything out about an hour ago. And now it's time to take care of you."

"But don't you worry," General Martin said. "You're going to live a long time. We will have a clown torture that will be grander than any other clown torture in history. It's going to be a roadshow! Your clown board will be on a semi. You'll tour the old South. Then you will be planted in the Parking Lot of Shame."

Mrs. Clownie held up the chainsaw. "At each stop on the tour, I will cut off one of your fingers. And then I'll cut out your tongue. Faxes should be seen. Not heard. And then I will cut off your arms. And then, after each show, we'll reattach everything. Of course, nothing will ever work as well as it used to. You'll be a serious freak. Your parts will be all crooked and mismatched. Every day, your pain will grow. We are talking serious pain and humiliation that will go on and on."

"Now, now, now," General Martin said. "Romulus is a Godless, soulless Fax, but I'm a good Christian." He eyed Purple up and down and licked his lips. "There is no reason to destroy valuable assets." He looked back at Romulus. "All you have to do is give me the code that TinKan's double gave you. Once we have that, we can reset the password. If you give it to us, you can all go free. I will drop all charges against you and reinstate you as a full-fledged surgeon."

"No," Mrs. Clownie said. "He killed my husband."

"Blessed are the peacemakers," General Martin said. "Let the one without sin shoot the first round of ammo." He rubbed his chin and looked at TinKan. "What do you say?"

"Romulus is a valued surgeon. I say let bygones be bygones."

"I'll reinstate you," General Martin said. "I'll give you a promotion and a twenty percent raise, and, as a bonus, I'll give you a free overhaul. I'll replace your central pump and give you a six-month free TruSnak™ coupon."

"And I will activate your pleasure circuits and enroll you in the pleasure unit of the month club," TinKan said. "All we want is the code."

Romulus's display displayed a warning in flashing red letters. *Total system failure imminent.*

JOAN jumped up and down. “Don’t believe a word they say.”

“Of course, I don’t believe them,” Romulus told her. “Tell me something I might be able to use.”

Mrs. Clownie crept forward to the edge of the assembly line. It was five feet high, so she was looking down at them. She raised her saw. Likewise, General Martin limped closer with a Fax prod.

“I searched your database,” JOAN said. “This is a standard assembly line without added security features. There are two buttons on it right below Mrs. Clownie’s foot. One is pressed in. That is the stop button. The other is the start button. Layla, it doesn’t look like anyone is paying too much attention to you. You are very quick. If you jump forward, you might be able to press the start button with your nose.”

“That is a great idea,” Romulus said. “It will create a diversion.”

“I can do it,” Layla said.

“And there is one other thing I found out,” JOAN said. “The dumb Faxes are all connected to the server. If you do a reset of the server, all the dumb Faxes will be disabled.”

“All right, we have a chance,” Romulus said. “Get ready, everyone. As soon as Layla jumps, we all start shooting. Purple and Cameron, you seek cover behind the posts under the assembly line and shoot from there. Layla, as soon as you start the assembly line, seek cover and wait for opportunities to pounce. I will disable the server. They won’t be expecting us to fight. Okay, on three. One.”

General Martin moved closer to Romulus.

“Two.”

Mrs. Clownie leaned down with the saw.

“Three.”

Layla catapulted into the start button, hitting it with her nose. The assembly line roared to life, lights flashing and gears and pulleys grinding and whirring. Mrs. Clownie teetered back and forth as the assembly line moved forward. She struggled to stay in place and maintain her balance as it rolled forward.

Romulus rammed the butt of his rifle against Martin's head, knocking him to the ground. With the bullets whizzing, he grabbed the grenades from Martin's belt, pulled the pins, and tossed them into the crowd as fast as he could.

One landed next to TinKan. He tried to grab it but couldn't because he only had one arm, and it exploded and knocked him to the ground.

Some of the Cowboys ran from the explosions and ran into the spinning saws of the dumb Faxes.

Mrs. Clownie leaned down and swiped at Romulus with the saw. He grabbed it and slashed her arm. She shrieked. Blood spurted everywhere.

"Kill him, kill him," she screamed, her half-severed arm hanging from her side as blood gushed.

The grenades exploded one after the other. Debris and shrapnel hit Romulus, but he stayed upright and shot Cowboys with the gun and slashed them with the saw.

Purple and Cameron fired at the Reals from behind the support beams in the assembly line.

General Martin propped himself up. Blood covered his face. He aimed a gun at Romulus, but Layla bit his arm, making him drop his weapon. He tried to kick her, but his peg leg came off, and he fell back.

The room was filled with smoke.

A warning flashed in his display. "One minute to system failure."

There was only one thing to do. He brought up his core settings and selected TruSnak™ reserve. One of the choices was "Release all reserves." He chose that option.

"Oh, my!" JOAN said.

"I have no choice."

"Warning," his display said. "If you proceed, your

system may not reboot."

He pressed it. Energy flooded through him, but it didn't provide as much of a jolt as he thought. Alligator AL's formulation was inferior, and the pump replacement would take time. He was in trouble.

He crawled forward under the smoke to the control panel. The Cowboys fired at him, but it was hard for them to see, and Purple and Cameron provided heavy cover fire.

One of the dumb Faxes jumped in front of him and brought his circular saw down toward Romulus's head. Romulus rolled away from him, stuck his gun through the exposed ribs onto the central pump, and fired. The bullet shattered the pump and sent parts, oil, and hydraulic fluid everywhere.

Romulus reached the control panel.

A Cowboy tried to stop him. Purple shot him, but he shot her point-blank in the chest, knocking her to the ground. A grenade exploded next to Cameron, blowing his feet off.

Martin had put his peg leg on and hobbled to Romulus. He stuck a Fax prod on his temple and pressed the trigger. Romulus shuddered in pain. "You have tried to destroy my life's work. Vengeance is mine sayeth the Lord. I am the right hand of the Father. And shall God not avenge His own elect who cry out day and night to Him, though He bears long covid with them? I tell you that He will avenge them speedily."

He hobbled back and forth in front of Romulus and drooled as he spoke.

"When the Son of Man comes, will He really find white people on the earth? Whoever kills any man shall surely be put to death. Whoever kills a Fax shall make it good, circuit for circuit. If a man causes disfigurement of his neighbor, so shall it be done to him—fracture for fracture, eye for eye, tooth for tooth. And whoever kills an animal shall restore it with ribeye steaks. But whoever disobeys a

Real shall be put to death by clown torture. You shall have the same law for the stranger and for one from your own country; for I am the Lord your God. Vengeance is Mine, and recompense; Their foot shall slip in due time; For the day of their calamity is at hand, And the things to come hasten upon them."

He dialed the Fax prod to heavy stun. The tip glowed. "The code. I want the code."

Layla was inching toward him.

"General Martin, I have a question for you," Romulus said. "If vengeance belongs to the Lord, then why are you passing judgment?"

"Because He has given me the power to do what needs to be done."

"But how do you know what God wants? Is it possible you could be wrong? I am not questioning the Lord. I'm wondering if maybe you got the wrong message. Maybe it has been the devil talking to you all this time."

The old man's face blanched red. "I'll show you God's will."

He started to press the prod onto Romulus's forehead, but Layla attacked, biting his ankle. He fell to the ground, and the prod rolled from his hand.

Purple raced forward and kicked General Martin in the head. He reeled back, and Layla picked up the prod in her mouth and stunned him.

Romulus crawled to the data entry keypad.

"No!" General Martin yelled.

Romulus entered the code and navigated to the central server. One of the Faxes swung his blade at him. Purple kicked him away. Another Fax swung at her, but Cameron crawled and tackled him. Purple kicked him in the head.

Romulus reached the reset button. If he hit it, everything in The Hospital would reboot. The surgery suites would lose power briefly. Patients might die. But it was certain that he and his cohorts would die if he didn't press the button.

More Faxes approached.

The system asked him to reenter the code. He did.

The assembly line stopped, and all the lights turned off.

CHAPTER THIRTY-FOUR

Alarms sounded. And air horns. The backup power came on after a few seconds.

All the dumb Faxes had fallen to the ground. Cameron kept shooting, killing the Cowboys one by one.

General Martin crawled toward the back, but the rolling chain-link gate stopped him. Layla moved up on one side; Purple moved up on the other. Romulus approached him straight on.

"Now, have a little mercy," General Martin said, pulling himself up to stand. "It's tough being a boss. Everybody's looking at you, expecting you to make the right decision. It's not easy. Particularly when you're trying to do the right thing for the Lord."

"Liar," Purple said. "You are selfish and used Faxes for your own needs. You deserve to suffer."

Suddenly, TinKan rose and stood behind General Martin.

"Well, thank God, the cavalry arrived," General Martin said with a smile.

"I'm right behind you," TinKan said. Slowly, he raised his rifle.

Romulus and Purple kept their guns trained on them. Layla growled and was ready to pounce.

TinKan didn't point his barrel at Romulus. He raised the muzzle until it was an inch from General Martin's head. Martin had his back to the Rogue and didn't see what was happening.

"Well, you're not so smart now, are you, Romulus?" Martin said. "Put your guns down, and we'll let all of you go free if you give us the code."

TinKan pulled the trigger and killed General Martin. Blood, gore, and pieces of his skull flew everywhere. His body slumped to the ground.

Purple let her gun fall to her side, and Layla sat back on her haunches.

"So, you were on our side all along," Romulus said.

TinKan put the muzzle of his gun on Purple's forehead. He fired, and the bullet cracked her skull open.

Then, he shot Layla.

TinKan walked up to Romulus and put the muzzle of his gun on Romulus's chest. "I was never on anyone's side. Only my own. You thought you were smart, didn't you? Well, you are smart. And you are courageous. But you have a fatal flaw. Do you know what that is?"

Romulus said nothing.

"Answer me. What is your fatal flaw?"

"I don't know."

"You are decent. That makes you a lost cause. But I wanted to know more about the factory and the Reals. And you proved remarkably useful in gathering information." He paused and laughed. "But you know what I wanted most of all?"

"No."

"I wanted your hands. I've wanted your hands for a long time. If you had followed orders and left Abraham in the suburbs, I might have saved you. You are the best surgeon, and you could have helped me. Think of what I could have done for you. All new lines. All new pumps. A ninety-five percent increase in efficiency. You would need less TruSnak™. A new battery. And consider your synthskin. Compare it to my skin. Feel my face and feel yours."

He leaned close, and Romulus felt it, then felt his own.

"See, mine is softer. Yours is harder and will soon become brittle. It will start to crack, and you will need complete resurfacing. And look at our eyes. See how mine are brighter than yours. You need new eyes, and you don't have any coin. You missed your chance. The Metroplex is going to help me. You wanted to help your friends. Look at them now. The dog is dead. The Purple freak has her head blown in half, and this freak Cameron has no feet. General Martin and I worked together for many years. We raided Corpus Christi periodically, and General Martin raided us. It was all planned and choreographed. But he got real cozy with the Metroplex and didn't tell me about that. It made me mad. So, I sent Remus."

"So, Remus betrayed me?"

"Remus was a fool. I sent him in to contact you. But then I got a little surprise. My double didn't understand it was all a con. He mounted a second attack without telling me. And that led to another misunderstanding with General Martin." He laughed. "My double was a Rogue who went rogue. Can you see the irony?"

"Yes, I can."

"I knew you would. Only a few can make it to the top. General Martin had what it took. I do, too. And you are also exceptional. You had the skills to make a difference. And now that Martin is out of the way, I take over everything. I hate Reals. They will only be laborers. Corpus Christi will be run by Faxes." He laughed uproariously. "There is just that one final thing I need from you. Or should I say two things?"

"My hands?"

"Yes, and your arms, too. Because of distributed processing, much of your surgical knowledge resides in your hands. They are valuable. I want them and might as well take the arms, too. I need one anyway, so I might as well take them both. It wouldn't look good to have two mismatched arms. And I want to look good. The Metroplex surgeons will cut them off and attach them to my body."

Layla spoke up in the metaverse. "I am not dead. I had a body plate on my stomach. Attack now."

Purple jumped to her feet. Even though the top half of her was destroyed, the bottom half worked fine. She kicked the gun from TinKan's hand.

Layla jumped on him and knocked him to the ground. Purple clamped her legs around his neck. Cameron crawled to him and grabbed his ankles.

TinKan could not fight all of them because he only had one arm. He dropped the Fax prod. Romulus picked it up, dialed it to full stun, and stuck it in TinKan's arm stump. He shoved it in all the way to the hilt and turned it on.

TinKan's body twitched and flexed as the electricity surged through it. His eyes bulged, and one eye burst. The synthskin on his shoulder bubbled. Smoke came out of his ears. Finally, the body settled.

Romulus was happy to see him dead but had no time to enjoy the victory. He was so weak that he fell to the ground. "I need TruSnak™ if I'm going to have enough strength to do the pump transplant. Can you drag one of the dumb Faxes over here so I can get some of his?"

Cameron crawled to the nearest one and pulled it, but his ankle assemblies started disintegrating. Purple helped by pushing it with one foot while balancing on the other. Layla helped, too, by pushing with her snout.

When they pulled it up next to him, Romulus tried to unscrew the dumb Fax's chest cover plate. But he was so weak, he couldn't. Cameron got it loose and then unscrewed Romulus's chest plate.

"Can you sit upright, sir?" Cameron asked. "You need to sit upright so I can pour the TruSnak™ into you."

He couldn't do it.

"Can you help me, Purple?" Cameron asked.

The bullet to her head had split her skull. The right side hung at an angle, and her right eye dangled from the socket. Hydraulic fluid was leaking through the split in her skull. It started dripping out of her left eye socket, too.

However, she managed to shove him into a sitting condition with her legs. Layla moved up behind and braced him.

Cameron poured the TruSnak™ into Romulus's well.

"Oh, that feels so good," Romulus said. "Now, I have to transplant Blonde's pump into me. I'll need some help."

With great effort, Cameron, Purple, and Layla rolled an external pump over to him. Cameron's legs were coming loose at the knees, a tangle of wires and hoses trailing out, leaving fluids and debris behind. Purple's left eyeball had fallen out of its socket because of the pressure from the hydraulic fluid. The split in her skull was growing, and Romulus could see her mouth and nose assemblies. The hole in her chest was getting bigger, too, and the slow leak of hydraulic fluid was starting to spurt. "Yes, I can do it," her mouth said. "Green Eggs and Ham, praise me, Jesus and Skidamarinkydo."

Cameron attached the hoses of the external pump to Romulus. When it powered up, Romulus felt energy surging through him.

He loosened the connectors and bolts on his old pump and pulled them loose. The pump was still welded to the center spine rod, but Cameron hadn't done a good job with the weld, and they pried it loose with a crowbar.

"Cameron, you'll have to hold Blonde's pump in position while I hook it up."

"All right. Yes, sir."

Romulus looked down into his chest cavity. "Layla, please give me a clamp."

She did, and he fastened the pump on his central spine rod.

"Bolts," he told Layla.

She picked them up with her mouth and put them in his hand. He screwed them in with a wrench and squirted the spine with ROBOT 60/60 to clean the rust off.

"Now a sponge."

She gave him one, and he wiped the fluid away. "Soldering iron."

She gave him one, and he laid a solder line around the pump. A weld would have been better, but the solder would hold for a while.

"Now disconnect me from the external pump."

Cameron did.

System functioning flashed in his display.

Romulus felt elated. Purple danced with her skull split down the center, each half dangling off the central supporting rod. "Gonna lay down my burden, Down by the riverside," she sang out loud repeatedly. Her speech assembly fell out, and it kept singing. "Oh me, oh my, cherry pie, cherry pie."

Romulus found some tubing and tied her head together so it wouldn't completely fall apart.

"We have to get out of here," Layla said. "The Metroplex Cowboys will come.

Cameron moaned. "Leave me here, Romulus. I have no legs. You must save yourself. Run."

"No, we all came in together. We all leave together."

He loaded Purple and Cameron onto a dolly and pulled them out of the factory.

"Here we go round the mulberry bush, the mulberry bush," Purple's speech assembly sang.

Romulus put it in his pocket.

"Leave that," Layla said. "If there are any Cowboys anywhere, they'll hear it.

"Hey diddle diddle, the cat and the fiddle," it sang, clattering in his pocket. "Mary had a little lamb, a little lamb."

"It is annoying," Layla said. "Leave it here."

"No, we came together, and we leave together with as many of our parts as we can. Besides, who knows what we're facing in the long term? We might need a speech assembly." He pulled it out of his pocket, opened the back of the assembly, and set it to mute. "There."

They moved down the hall. Emergency lights flickered. The heavy cart had a bad wheel, clanking as Romulus pulled it along. They took the hallway to an area above the freight entrance where Ryan and Abraham were supposed to be.

"Ryan, are you there?" he asked.

No answer. No sign of an avatar.

"Abraham, are you there?"

No answer. No sign of an avatar.

"We'll have to go down there," Romulus said. "We have no other choice."

"The elevator's not working," Layla said. "We'll have to use the stairs. Cameron will be hard enough to carry, but Purple is fighting you all the way. There is nothing left of her personality. We have to leave her."

"I can carry her."

"Wake up and smell the hydraulic fluid," JOAN said. "Your pleasure modules have never been properly activated, and your feelings are all mixed up. You like Purple, and you even like Layla."

"She is right," Layla said. "I, too, have been altered, and my feelings aren't quite right. I haven't been honest, Romulus. I have a husband, a coydog named Hercules."

"Hercules?"

"Yes, he's on a mission."

"I see. It is logical to assume that I am not properly processing my romantic feelings because I do not have activated pleasure modules. But it doesn't matter. We came together, and we're leaving together."

Purple got up from the dolly. She tried to dance but fell to the ground. Romulus threw her over one shoulder and Cameron over the other. Layla raced ahead to see what was happening, and Romulus carried squirming Purple and legless Cameron.

"The back door is open," Layla said when he reached the ground floor. "There's no sign of the van, Abraham, or Ryan."

CHAPTER THIRTY-FIVE

"Layla, scout around outside," Romulus said. "See what you can find."

Purple wouldn't stay still on his back. He wondered if he should let her go. There was so little left of what she had been. Even if he had proper equipment and supplies to repair her, there would be nothing of her personality.

In her present state, she was a liability.

Even so, he couldn't let her go. Nor could he let Cameron go. How odd. Cameron had a working head and chest but no legs. Purple had legs, but her head was so severely damaged that it would soon corrode and ultimately disintegrate. What a statement about the nature of life.

Her speech assembly was in his pocket. It was set to mute, but the teeth kept chattering. It popped out of his pocket and landed on the ground. Its teeth chattered, and then it stopped and faced him with an open mouth.

"I'll get us out of here," Romulus said, unsure if the mouth could understand him. "And then we'll fix you."

The teeth chattered frantically, and the assembly bounced all around him.

"Oh, my," Cameron said. "That mouth has a mind of its own. If you can understand us, then stay still. There is no way we'll get out of here if you cause us to be discovered."

This had an impact. The teeth stopped chattering, and Purple quit squirming so much on his back. It was like the teeth and the body were communicating with each other.

Romulus picked up the teeth, put them back in his pocket, and proceeded down the hall. He stepped out the open back door onto the loading dock.

The truck pulled up to them.

Abraham yelled out the window to them. "Hurry. The Metroplex Cowboys are right behind us. We have to get out of here."

"It makes me sappy to the maxie to see a Faxie," Ryan said. "I might react to the fact with a pat on the back."

Romulus loaded Purple and Cameron. "I understand if you have to leave me," Cameron said. "I am not worth anything."

"You are worth more than you know. Nobody gets left behind."

He looked around for Layla. Where was she?

"We got to flee if we want to be free," Ryan said.

"Yes, the Metroplex Cowboys are close," Abraham said.

Suddenly, Layla raced around the corner and jumped into the van. "The Metroplex 4X4s are approaching from several directions. We are surrounded."

Before Ryan could drive away, a group of trucks blocked them both front and back.

It looked hopeless, but drones suddenly appeared and fired on the 4X4s.

"Go," Romulus said.

Ryan screeched around the trucks.

"Go down Ocean Drive," JOAN said.

Ryan sped forward, but a group of 4X4s pulled

behind them, firing their guns. The drones came in low and drove the trucks back.

One drone flew alongside them, slowing and circling. *Romulus, requesting permission to enter your metaverse.*

He looked at Ryan. "You're the one who told me about the drones. What do you think?"

"They are the real deal. They helped you escape the scrape on the stage."

Romulus granted permission. The avatar had eyes where the drone's windows were, and the wings moved like arms. "I represent the Free Shania Society. We are a secret group of Faxes that opposed TinKan. We have just freed Shania and many other victims of clown torture. We are evacuating Corpus Christi. We will provide air support for your travels if you provide medical support to us."

Romulus looked to the group. "What do you think?"

"Yes, we agree," they all said.

"What are you going to do with Cameron and Purple?" JOAN said. "He has no legs, and she has no head."

"I will merge them," Romulus said. "I will combine her bottom with his top."

"But you'll create a freak."

"We're all freaks."

The teeth chattered in his pocket.

"And we'll find a place for Purple's speech assembly. Everyone deserves a voice."

Romulus looked at the spare parts in the back of the van. He could rebuild everything if he could get the tools and equipment.

"Where are we going?" Layla asked.

"North. Maybe Chicago. We'll have to find TruSnak™ and supplies along the way."

Ryan brightened. "I know a place. It's ace, and no

one can trace our face. The key is Albuquerque."

They sped down Ocean Drive past the deteriorating buildings as the drones flew alongside.

THE END OF BOOK ONE
OF
ROMULUS ESCAPES

www.ingramcontent.com/pod-product-compliance
Lightning Source LLC
Chambersburg PA
CBHW030334310726
48979CB00001B/26
9781733469678